Playpen

Impulsively, she stepped inside the cabin. She glanced around. She was alone — except for a baby. It was a rather bald, red-faced infant standing at the rail of a crib as ancient as the playpen. When it caught sight of her, its noises escalated into howls. While the baby cried, it shook the bars of its bed with white-knuckled fists.

"I know just how you feel," Laurel said, moving toward the crib.

The child bounced up and down. It continued to cry. Laurel put her hands on her hips. Then warily, she stepped forward and touched the child on its head. Instead of being comforted, the baby wailed even louder.

"Now what?" Laurel asked herself.

But even as she posed the question, she knew what she had to do.

Other **Apple** paperbacks
you will enjoy:

Truth or Dare
  by Susan Beth Pfeffer

Starting with Melodie
  by Susan Beth Pfeffer

Adorable Sunday
  by Marlene Fanta Shyer

A Season of Secrets
  by Alison Cragin Herzig
  and Jane Lawrence Mali

Starstruck
  by Marisa Gioffre

The Trouble with Soap
  by Margery Cuyler

Baby-Snatcher

Susan Terris

AN **APPLE** PAPERBACK

SCHOLASTIC INC.
New York Toronto London Auckland Sydney

For Maggie—welcome to the Terris family . . .

ISBN 0-590-43756-9

12 11 10 9 8 7 6 5 4 3 2 1   0 1 2 3/9

Printed in the U.S.A.   01

ONE

JUNE

June never changed. Someone was canoeing on the lake. A man — stroking Indian-style, so there was no drip, drip, drip sound as he feathered his paddle. Clouds, reflecting on the water's surface, created an illusion of a flotilla of icebergs.

Laurel stood in the wet grass at the edge of the beach. Holding her breath, she watched the canoe slice in and out of sun, ice, and shadow. Who, she wondered, was in the aluminum shell? Anyone that knew how quickly a Minnesota squall could appear wouldn't be so far from shore. Then, forgetting the paddler, Laurel exhaled. It was morning, it was summer, and she was back at Hoop Lake.

She started walking again. Burrs scratched at her ankles. Dew seeped through the toes of her canvas sneakers. Instead of feeling thirteen and about to enter high school, she felt odd. Looking at the lake she seemed to see a collage of the summers of her life, which made her feel all previous ages yet none, unreal and insubstantial as the phantom icebergs floating on the water.

Laurel stepped from the grass onto a nearby path. Then for a moment she paused. She was waiting for something to happen. She longed for excitement or summer romances — stories to tell her friends back home in Creve Coeur. Nothing ever happened to her at Hoop Lake. It was a place where time seemed suspended.

With a sigh, Laurel turned from the lake. As the path wound away from the shore and through the woods, she followed it hypnotically. She was glad to be out of the house where her brother still slept. On her own. Alone. Some place she didn't have to prove to anyone that she deserved to be part of the illustrious Tavrow family. A place she didn't have to struggle to be smart or pretty or popular.

Thinking about these struggles made her wince. Her friends at home wanted to be independent from their parents. Laurel did, too. But she had two sets of parents to contend with. Her mother and father told her what to do, but so did her sister and brother.

In one way or another, the four of them were always criticizing, implying that she was an impractical dreamer.

Annoyed, Laurel tried to forget family and concentrate on the present. She felt her dark-blond braids flop against her shoulders. A crow cawed. The shadowed woods chilled her bare legs. She looked up, remembering a time when the trees around her had names, a time when they were part of Druidworld. She missed Druidworld. Pretend worlds were easier than the real one. Now she was supposed to be growing up, leaving make-believe behind. And she was. The Druid names had slipped away, except for one — the name of the gnarled pine looming before her: King Tarik. Remembering gave her a sense of peace and lightness.

She glided forward, made a bow. "All hail, King Tarik," she intoned. "All hail, King of — "

Before she could finish her greeting, peals of laughter filled the air. They were fiendish, unearthly. A hundred voices seemed to be mocking her. Trying to blot out the din, she closed her eyes and pressed her hands against her ears.

Suddenly the laughter stopped. For a moment, the woods were silent. Then she heard another laugh, a familiar whinnying sound, followed by a voice. "It works. It really works! Thank you, Pokey."

Laurel opened her eyes. "Spencer Harrison! I should have known!" She laughed at the tall, thin, freckled boy who stood in the path before her. "I hate you. I really do."

"I bet you say that to all the guys in St. Louie," the boy said. "Well, look at you. Look at little Laurel." He gestured. "I like them."

Instinctively, Laurel clutched her arms across her chest. Spencer snickered. "Not those," he said, reaching out to pull on her braids. "These. Speaking of *those*, though — how is your sister? Jessica, beautiful Jessica — the love of my life."

"Shut up, Spence." Laurel stepped off the path and started to walk past him, but he caught hold of her braids again.

"I understand your folks aren't coming till the end of August. Momma says Jessica and Miles are taking turns baby-sitting you. You're so lucky. I'd like to have Jessica for my sitter. I'd like to have folks who jetted around the world. So tell me about their trip and about Jessie — *all* about her. After all, she's only twenty-two, right? And that's not too old for me."

Laurel frowned. "She's twenty-three. Besides, Miles is here now," she answered mechanically. Everyone asked about her parents' travels or about Jessie and Miles. Her parents were in Sri Lanka, where her father was a business consultant and her mother was doing research for a magazine article. Jessica, who was in architecture school, and Miles, who was pre-med at Stanford, were sharing a summer job in their father's office. Every two or three weeks they planned to trade places so Laurel had someone to stay with her at Hoop Lake.

"Is Jessica still beautiful?" Spencer asked.

"Yes, beautiful and perfect," Laurel told him. "Miles is, too."

Spencer let go of her hair. "I didn't ask about Miles. I don't have a crush on *him*."

Laurel stepped back onto the path. She turned toward the Tavrow house. It wasn't nine o'clock yet and her morning was ruined. She was going to go back to bed. Maybe she'd stay in bed for the summer. Or forever. She had spent time with Spencer every summer since she was a baby, explored with him, played Druid with him. But that was over now. He was fifteen, nearly sixteen. He and his mother, Annie, lived at the lake. Annie operated a gas station and worked as a winter caretaker for the homes on Hoop Lake. She was okay, but Laurel no longer had any use for her son.

As Laurel began to stride away from him, however, the terrible laughter started again. "Spencer!" she cried. All of a sudden it was clear. She hadn't imagined that noise. It was another one of his gadgets.

"It works," he said, bending down and fiddling with something hidden in tufts of grass. "You see, you broke the electric eye, and it set off this tape recorder. But listen, Pokey, if you'll come with me, I have something else to show you."

Laurel groaned. She hated that nickname. It was bad enough at home. No one outside her family used it — no one except Spencer, of course. Spencer, who'd known her since she was in diapers.

"My car. Come on, girl. You're getting kind of cute, you know. So, come on — come see my car."

"I am not interested in cars," Laurel said, turning back to glare at his pointy-nosed face. "I am not interested in you. Therefore, I am not interested in any car belonging to you."

By now she was so angry that she no longer felt like returning home. Spencer was an idiot. He cared about breasts and machines, yet he didn't know a thing about romance. *Boys. Boyfriends.* Laurel's Creve Coeur classmates were desperate for them. They thought that having one was the way to be grown-up and independent. But Laurel was self-conscious and tongue-tied around boys. Besides, she didn't want a boyfriend. Particularly if it was someone like Spencer.

"And you can do me a big favor, Spencer. Don't talk to me now, next week, next month. Or ever."

Spencer flashed a sly grin in her direction. "You always had a sweet heart and a sweet tongue. Hey, would you come to the drive-in with me some time? What do you say? How about it, Queen Ingrid?"

Queen Ingrid. Her Druid name. Laurel refused to look up at him. She stared through the middle stripe on his red-and-white T-shirt. Then, pushing him aside, she started off down the path. As she did, the laughter rose up around her again. She had broken his electric eye one more time.

Seething, she strode past the Harrison house, following the path as it led around a marsh, then out again toward the shore. Once or twice, she stopped to see if Spencer was following her, but he wasn't. She almost wished he were. She ached for an excuse to beat him up as she used to do when they were kids.

With clenched fists, she forged ahead. The grass was higher now, almost up to her waist. Though she seemed to be wandering aimlessly, she was heading for the abandoned trapper's cabin at the edge of the Harrison property. It had been one of her favorite places at Hoop Lake. Not hers and Spencer's — just hers.

She skirted around the back edge of the cabin, coming out of the woods and into a clearing. In a moment, she'd strip down to her bathing suit and take a swim in the private bay below the cabin. Then she'd lie on the sand pretending she was invisible, staring at the clouds and lake until her mind was blank. As she anticipated this, she could feel her anger begin to slip away.

A curtain flapped at a side window of the cabin. Laurel ignored it. She was thinking of the summer stretching out ahead of her. A long, uneventful one. But then, as she pivoted around the front corner of the cabin, she walked into an obstacle. Something wooden with bars. It was a small cage.

No, it wasn't. It was an old-fashioned playpen. A baby's pen with rows of pink, blue, and yellow ABC's turning somersaults in the wind that had begun to riffle the surface of the lake. She stared at the playpen. What was an antique playpen or any playpen doing parked in front of her cabin? The cabin wasn't hers, of course. It belonged to the Harrisons, but it hadn't been lived in for years. Laurel peered from side to side. Under a clump of trees, she saw an unfamiliar truck with a dent in one fender.

Spencer knew that she hung out here. "Why didn't he tell me?" she muttered. "Why didn't he?"

Suddenly remembering the curtain swaying in the window, she spun around and faced the front of the cabin. The door was wide open. Goose bumps prickled her scalp and raced down her arms. She wondered if she should sneak off before she was discovered. Then, looking down at the empty playpen, she shook her head. The people in the cabin had a baby. She didn't particularly like babies, but she was curious, inclined to welcome anything that promised to add interest to a monotonous summer.

Stalling, she smoothed out her T-shirt, yanked at her cutoffs so they didn't ride up her bottom. "Hello," she called. "Is anybody home?"

TWO

Laurel expected a smiling young mother to appear in the doorway of the cabin with a skillet in hand and a fat baby on one hip. But no one came. "Hello," she called, walking up the front steps. Halting at the threshold, she peered inside. She saw books, clothes strewn about, smelled the damp, moldy odor of cushions and mattresses that had been stored unused for a long time.

"Hello," she repeated. Tentatively, she knocked.

There was still no answer. Nothing more suspicious than the wind had been responsible for the flapping curtain. Shrugging, she turned away. As she did, she thought she heard a puppy whimpering. She stood and listened. Soon she realized that she wasn't listening to an animal but to a baby — the baby that belonged to the playpen.

"Hello," she called out, as she knocked again.

She waited for sounds of activity from within, but she heard nothing except little cries and an unfamiliar rattling. Impulsively, she stepped inside the cabin. She glanced around. She was alone — alone except for a baby. It was a rather bald, red-faced infant standing at the rail of a crib as ancient as the playpen. When it caught sight of her, its noises escalated into howls. While the baby cried, it shook the bars of its bed with white-knuckled fists.

"I know just how you feel," Laurel said, moving toward the crib.

The child bounced up and down. It continued to cry. Laurel put her hands on her hips. Then warily, she stepped forward and touched the child on its head. Instead of being comforted, the baby wailed even louder.

"Now what?" Laurel asked herself.

But even as she posed the question, she knew what she had to do. So, awkwardly, she reached out and lifted the child into her arms. The baby's body was rigid. It kept howling. Laurel, acting with instinct instead of experience, patted its back, nudged her nose against one soft, damp cheek.

Gradually the baby began to relax. When

the cries had subsided into choked whimpers,
Laurel realized that it wasn't only the child's
cheek that was damp.

"Poor thing," Laurel said, bouncing the
baby up and down. "Who would do such a
thing — leave you to get as moldy as the rest
of this place?"

Laurel was pleased that the baby was
quiet, but she felt nervous. Everything
seemed unreal. Something dramatic was happening to her. People wrote newspaper articles about abandoned babies. Swaying back
and forth, she tried to decide what to do.
Then suddenly she knew. If this was an abandoned baby, she had to rescue it.

Quickly she looked around. She stepped
onto the screened porch that ran across the
back of the cabin. First, she caught sight of
tools and a series of small clay figures. Next,
she glimpsed a woman sitting there. As she
drew back, she realized that she had seen only
an unfinished carving of a woman. She looked
again. There was something unsettling about
the look on the woman's face. Laurel shivered.
She turned away from the statue and tightened her grip on the baby.

The baby protested by beginning to howl
again. "Sorry, kid, sorry," Laurel said apologetically. "But listen, I'm going to make it
better — all better. I promise."

Moving hastily, Laurel put the baby back in the crib. She rummaged about until she uncovered a carton of paper diapers. Then she stripped the wet clothing and diaper off the infant. "So you're a girl," Laurel commented when that fact became obvious.

As Laurel struggled to wrap the baby in fresh diapers and a blanket, the child looked up at Laurel with frowning curiosity. She seemed neither pleased nor alarmed to find herself being handled by a stranger.

Laurel, trying to stay calm, kept on talking. "You're no great beauty, of course, but maybe it will be better when you grow hair." She paused, clicked the baby's heels together. "Okay, okay — be patient, I'm almost finished. There, there, and there!"

Next, grabbing both the child and a blanket, she hurried from the cabin. She had taken only three steps when something wooden knocked against her ankles and clattered to the ground. At the same instant, a pair of hands reached out and took the baby. Then a coarse white mesh fell over her head, trapping her.

"What's going on here?" a man's voice demanded. "Who are you? Why are you making off with my daughter?"

Laurel clawed at the mesh. She smelled fish — dead fish. She was enveloped in a net that had been used to seine them. Frightened, she struggled to free herself. When the net fell to the ground, however, she was too shaky to run.

"What's going on here?" the voice repeated. Laurel raised her eyes. There before her, holding the baby, was a stocky, red-bearded young man.

Laurel looked down. A paddle lay at her feet. "The canoe," she said slowly. "You must be the man in the canoe."

"Oh, yes, she's a bright one, this little kidnapper."

Laurel flicked her braids behind her shoulders. Instead of being scared, she was indignant. At Spencer for starting her day off so badly; at a man who would leave his baby alone, then terrify her by throwing a fishnet over her head.

"You monster! Why did you leave this baby alone here? That's awful, dangerous. Why —"

"Okay, okay — shush. Calm down. Look, I went out in the canoe because Doe was still sleeping. The minute she started to cry, I raced right in. The way sound carries in the morning on a lake like this, I could have heard her hiccup. Besides, why am I bothering to explain this to *you*? You're the one who tried to sneak off with her. What *were* you doing?"

"I was saving her," Laurel answered. "But what about you — you and that net?"

The man shrugged. "I was saving her, too. And the net seemed like an appropriate way to treat someone who'd try to snatch my baby."

Laurel wanted to stay angry, but she could not seem to do it. She felt young, silly, powerless. Besides, the baby, who had not smiled even once at her, was smiling at the man, tugging happily on his curly red beard.

Laurel leaned her head to one side. "She's yours?"

"That's what I said." The man shifted the baby to a better position. "You're my girl, aren't you, honey?"

As Laurel tried to decide what to do, she licked her lips. Then, begrudgingly, she smiled. "I'm Laurel Tavrow," she said, sticking out her hand.

After the man had examined her for an instant, he freed his right hand, extending it to meet hers. "Ivan," he said. "And this is my daughter, Doe. Are you from the peeled-bark lodge?"

She shook her head. "No, that's the nuns."

"The nuns?" he asked.

"The Sisters of Hope. They're teaching nuns, and they have their retreats there. We're the white place between them and the

Harrisons." That took care of all the houses at the east side of Hoop Lake. The north and south shores were rocky and uninhabited. The rest of the people who had houses on the lake lived a mile across in the southwestern bay.

"And was it the sisters I heard cackling a while ago? You could hear that laughing everywhere."

"The sisters?" Laurel said, chuckling as she remembered Spencer's tape recorder. "No, that was something Spencer rigged up."

"Spencer?"

"Spencer Harrison."

"Oh, Annie's son. The nosy, freckled wimp."

Laurel laughed. She liked hearing Spencer referred to that way.

"I'm her tenant," Ivan explained. "Doe and I are renting this place for the summer. Just for the summer, though. During the school year, I'm an art teacher at a college in the Twin Cities. But what I really am is a sculptor."

"That's nice," Laurel said, remembering the half-carved statue on its porch.

"Most of the time." As Ivan lingered speaking with Laurel, Doe began to fuss again. Ivan bounced her but showed no inclination to do anything else to soothe her.

"She looks hungry," Laurel said.

"She is, but she can wait a minute," Ivan replied. "Can't you, love? She'll wait, because we always have our breakfast together, don't we, Doe?"

Laurel backed up a few steps. "Well, I ought to be going. But she does look hungry, you know."

Ivan smiled. He had a V-shaped gap between his front teeth. He wasn't handsome exactly. Not tall and even-featured like her brother, Miles, but all right with his brownish hair, red beard, and square-shouldered build. He was wearing paint-stained Levi's and a blue work shirt. "You an expert in these matters, Laurel?"

"What matters?"

"The care and feeding of babies?" As he spoke, he rummaged in his pocket and produced something that looked like a dog biscuit. He put it gently into Doe's hand. "There. Now you chew on that, ducky, while I talk with this baby expert."

Laurel twisted her hands together behind her back. "Look, I'm no expert. I — "

"But you do know *something* about babies, don't you? A coincidence, I suppose, having you show up. You see, I'm looking for someone reliable to baby-sit. Would you be interested?"

Laurel raised her eyebrows. Ivan's question had caught her off guard. She thought for a moment. Baby-sitting would break up the monotony of the summer, but she wasn't sure. "What about your wife? Wouldn't she want to meet me?"

Ivan stroked his beard. He gave Doe a juicy kiss on the back of her neck. "My wife's not here," he said. "We're separated."

"I see," Laurel answered, straining to use her most adult voice.

"Do you?" He looked at her quizzically.

"No," she confessed, "I'm not sure I do."

"Well then," Ivan said, turning toward the cabin, "I'll admit to you that I'm not sure I understand it, either. Sometimes, though, life seems like a vast maze where you just have to keep moving to stay away from the Minotaur. And, yes, you're right. It is breakfast time. We should eat now. You're welcome to stay, if you'd like. And I meant what I said about sitting for Doe."

Laurel considered the offers for a moment — both of them. "No breakfast," she said. She wasn't sure about the baby-sitting, either, but it was tempting. She could get to know a sculptor. That would give her something to talk about when she went back home. He seemed interesting, too. She wondered what he meant about the maze and the Minotaur.

While she mulled this over, Ivan spoke again. "I'd like to see it in a French braid," he said.

"What?" she asked.

"Your hair. Instead of pigtails."

Laurel reached up and tugged at one braid.

"A French braid — over the top and down the back. I'll show you. If — or when — you come to sit. I like you, Laurel. And I always trust my first instincts about a person. So, if you like me, if you like Doe . . . come any morning at ten. Or before, if you want. I'm flexible. Keep track of your hours and I'll pay you."

Laurel felt almost as if she were sleep-walking. She was nodding, as if she were agreeing to be Doe's baby-sitter even when she hadn't made up her mind. Then, the next thing she knew, she turned off on the path that led through the woods.

"The maze and the Minotaur?" she asked herself as she made her way back down the path. "I wish I — "

Her wish, however, was silenced by peals of raucous laughter. Spencer's tape recorder had struck again. The whole time she'd been at the cabin with Ivan he'd probably been spying on them, listening to their conversation.

She wanted to scream at Spencer, but she managed to control herself. The best way she could think of to avoid him was to spend June, July, and August hanging out at the trapper's cabin.

"Geek!" she muttered. Then she used Ivan's word for Spencer: "Wimp!"

Feeling suddenly superior, Laurel walked on. Intrigued, imagining new and exciting possibilities for her summer, she willed herself to ignore the demonic voices that echoed in the woods behind her.

THREE

Laurel gazed at Ivan's sculpture. The woman appeared to be holding something invisible in her arms. Frowning, Laurel examined the way the carved figure rose out of its block of reddish wood. Because the woman's lower body was only roughly formed, she seemed almost imprisoned. Laurel sighed.

"A heavy sigh," Ivan commented. "Now sit still, will you? If you keep moving, I'll never get this right."

Laurel straightened her head. Ivan continued working. "Yes, better," he said. "So why did you sigh?"

"Because she — your woman — looks so sad."

"That she does. You are perceptive, Laurel. But stop distracting me so we can finish before Doe wakes up."

Doe was napping in the playpen, her thumb

tucked in her mouth, her bottom sticking up into the air. Ivan had put her into a shady spot where she wouldn't get sunburned. Ivan's sculpture and the table to which it was bolted had been moved from the screened porch to a bare spot in front of the cabin.

Laurel had waited several days before she'd come back to offer to baby-sit. She'd spent those days lying in the sun, swimming to the sandbar, watching for glimpses of Ivan paddling the canoe in and out of his cove. At last, overcoming her misgivings about caring for a small child, she'd retraced her route to the cabin.

Ivan seemed to be expecting her, and yet he didn't ask what had taken so long. Instead, he looked at her thoughtfully. She felt herself flush. She had dressed up for him — at least, she'd done her best within the limits of the clothes she had at Hoop Lake. She was wearing white jeans with a pink shirt tied at the midriff. Her hair hung loose on her shoulders.

After a moment, Ivan sprang into action. "Sit there. And shush, because Doe's sleeping. Yes, right. Now, don't move."

Flattered, Laurel did as he said. She sat on an old stump, her ankles crossed, waiting for him to produce a pad and begin to draw her picture. What Ivan had in mind, though, was slightly different. Before she knew what was happening, he produced a large blue comb from one of his pockets.

Then, with a few deft strokes, he separated her hair into the strands necessary for the French braid he had promised. She wasn't sure why she sat and let him work on her that way, yet she didn't protest.

When he finished, he backed off to admire what he had accomplished. "Splendid," he said. "I have done a first-rate transformation on you. You look like a different woman."

Gingerly, Laurel patted the unfamiliar ridge over the top of her head. The single braid down the middle of her back felt thick and substantial — more important, more grown-up than her usual summer pigtails. "Thank you," she said hesitantly. "Yes . . . well, but . . . where, where did you learn to do this?"

Ivan picked up a chisel and flicked it lightly against the arm of his woman. A paper-thin chip fell, joining others on the ground below. "Allison," he answered, shaving off another sliver of wood. "Doe's mother taught me."

Laurel thought maybe she shouldn't ask about Doe's mother, so she questioned Ivan about the baby. "How old is she? And her name. Is Doe her real name?"

"Nine months. She'll be a year old on the twelfth of September. And, well, no — Doe's not her real name. Allison named her Saskia. But that's such a mouthful. And besides, I think — around the eyes — she looks rather like a startled deer."

Laurel thought about a woman named Allison who had taught her husband to braid her hair, who had given birth to a baby, then separated from her husband. She tried to imagine what Allison would look like. Lean maybe and serious like Doe, only with hair. Maybe Allison had been the model for the statue poised before her. Laurel was drifting, picturing Ivan and Allison rocking Doe between them. Between them because, after all, a baby needed a father and a mother.

Allison. Laurel thought she might like being a young mother with a beautiful name like that. Allison, Allison — as the name tumbled in her head, she imagined a combination of the involved, interested person she'd like to be. Different from her own critical, too busy mother. Different from Jessica, too.

Ivan spoke, but she didn't hear what he had said. "What?" she asked.

"I said — how do you feel about trees? Like the maple next to the porch. We could climb it, get a crow's-nest view of the lake. What do you think?"

Startled, Laurel frowned. "You mean now?"

Tree climbing was not one of her favorite activities. Going up was usually fine. But then, looking out made her feel dizzy. And coming down she always felt shaky, uncertain of her footing. She didn't, however, want to admit this to Ivan.

"Of course, I mean now. Come on. I'll give you a leg up."

"Well. . . ."

"Why not?" Ivan asked enthusiastically. "Don't over analyze things — *do* them. Don't just think — act! It would be an adventure. I like adventures, don't you? Look, we could even take Doe up — strapped on my back. Sort of Swiss Family Robinson."

Gazing up at the tree, Laurel remembered the fishnet Ivan had thrown over her. That was a kind of game, like tree climbing. A game or an adventure. He liked adventure. Swiss Family Robinson, he'd said. Family. She could imagine Ivan up in the tree, swaying there with Doe and with a woman named Allison, but she couldn't picture herself. It didn't seem right. She could only imagine Ivan beckoning as a shadowy Allison rocked her child.

"Laurel!"

"Huh?"

"Where are you? What *are* you thinking about?"

Laurel licked her lips. "About your wife," she answered slowly. Then she squinted at Ivan, focusing in on what she really wanted to ask. "Why didn't she keep Doe?"

Ivan put down one chisel and took up another. He shrugged. "All right, we won't climb the tree. Instead, we're going to have an inquisition. So who is it that wants to know? Your parents? No — they're away, aren't they? Annie says you're with your brother. Well, no matter. I don't mind. Allison's in Minneapolis. She's a geriatric nurse. Because she works a night shift, it's hard for her — but I'm a teacher, and I have three months off. Makes sense. Right?"

Doe stirred in the playpen. She rolled over on her back and stretched in much the same way that Laurel's cat did after a nap. Laurel stood up and went over to the edge of the playpen. She waved at the baby, but Doe's only response was a suspicious frown. As Laurel stood there, Ivan dropped his tools and bounded forward. He scooped up his daughter and spun around with her. For her father, Doe smiled and gurgled softly. "Be-be-be-be."

Laurel chuckled. Ivan looked almost like a teenager as he waltzed about with the baby.

Ivan stopped spinning and looked at her. "What's so funny?"

Laurel leaned her head to one side. "I don't know. Just, I guess, that — right now — you look so young, younger than Miles."

"Miles?"

"My brother — the one who's up here with me. He's twenty-one."

"Only twenty-one?" Ivan asked, making faces at Doe, letting her tug at his nose. "Well, he's still a boy. I am already an old man of twenty-six."

"Sometimes," Laurel said wistfully, "I wish I were twenty-six and could skip the next ten or twelve years."

"Why?" Ivan asked, reaching into a box and producing a fresh diaper for Doe. He plopped her down on the stump Laurel had vacated and began to change her. "Why rush it?"

Laurel considered his question. "Because . . ." she began slowly, "school, college — it seems so hard. Making decisions, figuring out what I'm going to do. And the people part. For me, at least. I'm not like Miles or Jessie."

"Jessie?"

"My sister. She and Miles are special and talented. And I'm just me. I mean, I'm not very anything. So I dream sometimes about skipping it all."

Ivan sat Doe on the stump and clapped her hands together. "Pattycake, pattycake," he chanted. Then, after a moment, he turned back to Laurel. "There's nothing wrong, you know, with being a dreamer. I'm a dreamer. But if you're going to dream, Laurel, be a visionary. Be bold. Let the adrenaline pump, so you know what it feels like to be truly alive."

"Mmm . . ." Laurel mused, unsure of what he meant, yet impressed by the fiery tone in his voice.

"Besides, you *are* special, Laurel. Everyone's special in one way or another."

"Not me. I'm not."

Leaning forward, Ivan smiled. "Caterpillars," he commented, "have a way of turning into butterflies. Maybe you're not eating the right leaves."

FOUR

As Laurel headed through the woods, she thought about Ivan and what he had said about caterpillars. She had asked him a lot of questions. He had answered them thoughtfully, as he had danced with Doe in the clearing in front of the cabin.

But he had not asked her questions — even her age. He simply accepted her. She wasn't used to that. There was something magical about Ivan. He was energetic, unusual. He cast a spell, so that when he made a casual suggestion, she found herself eager to please him. And then, almost before she knew what had happened, she was marching along with a surprisingly heavy baby strapped in a carrier on her back.

Ivan had told her to be careful — not to let Doe out of her sight. He had packed a paper bag with diapers, clothes, a bottle, and a supply of dog biscuits — which had turned out to be sugarless baby cookies. He had also made her promise not to take Doe where she'd be around a lot of people.

"Babies are delicate," he warned. "Especially Doe. And I don't want her to pick up a cold or any other germs."

Laurel took him at his word. She would be careful of the child. She was terrified, she discovered, to be left alone with her. But she didn't intend to stay away from people. She couldn't. She headed straight toward her house. She had to ask Miles for a favor.

Absorbed, she was skirting the Harrison driveway when Spencer's voice bit into her. "Well, look at you," he said. "So that's where you've been keeping yourself."

He was bent over the back end of a battered-looking VW Beetle. Laurel kept on walking. She hadn't gotten very far, however, before Spencer loped up behind her. "What are you doing with the baby?"

"What does it look like?"

Spencer scratched his head. "Come on, Laurel. Ease up. You look pretty. Real pretty. Like you're all dressed up for a party or something," he said, gesturing at her clothes and hair.

Laurel groaned. Spencer and his compliments were not something she wanted. "Go 'way, Spence," she growled. "I'm baby-sitting. For Ivan — and the baby's not supposed to get near other people."

"Why not, little mother? What's so special? Funny baby, anyway. *So* serious. And that Ivan — he's kind of a hippie, isn't he? Mom says he's secretive. He may like you, but he grumbles when I'm around. I think he's a creep."

"Leave me alone," Laurel said. "Please — just this once. You're the creep around here. If Ivan says Doe is delicate, I do as he says. Because I'm working this summer, which is more than I can say for you."

"Me!" Spencer exclaimed. "I work every day putting this car into running condition — today I'm doing the carburetor. Then every night I'm at the station, almost all year round, so don't talk to me about working, summer girl."

Laurel felt the well-deserved sting of his statements. She had never had any job before, but she couldn't seem to control the sarcastic tone in her voice.

"Car? So why are you wasting your days fooling with a car when you're not even old enough to drive?"

"Maybe not in Missouri, where you live,

but Minnesota's a farm state. I got a special farm license — for going to school and for driving tractors."

"Is that a tractor?" she inquired as she tried to ignore the fact that Doe was pulling on the end of her braid.

Spencer flipped one hand in her direction and yanked her hair away from the baby. Doe started to howl. "What did you do *that* for?" Laurel asked excitedly.

Rolling his eyes, Spencer gave her hair another tug. "Because she was *chewing* on it, Pokey."

"Don't call me that."

Laurel jumped up and down awkwardly as she spoke. Doe was crying with no sign of letting up. Laurel didn't know what to do. In fact, she had no idea how to lift the baby from the carrier into her arms. Ivan had strapped her in, and Laurel had been so nervous that it had never occurred to her that she didn't know how to get the child out again.

"What's its name?" Spencer called, obviously amused at the crying baby and at Laurel's predicament.

"*Her* name," Laurel called back, swaying from side to side to see if that would comfort the squalling child, "is Doe."

"Don't you know how to keep her quiet?"

"No," Laurel confessed. "This was a terrible mistake. I shouldn't have taken her. I'm going back."

"Don't. Wait," Spencer insisted, moving behind Laurel. "I'll help. Here. Okay, kid, come to Uncle Spence."

Spencer slipped Doe from the carrier and slung her into Laurel's arms like a sack of potatoes. Being tossed around silenced Doe. She was hiccuping, but not crying anymore. Then Spencer took the bag of supplies from Laurel's left hand and wedged them into the carrier. She was grateful that he had helped solve her predicament, but she didn't intend to admit it.

Instead, she nodded curtly and started off toward her house. "See you," she said. That was the most she could manage.

"Hey, Lau-rel," he said.

"What?" she answered begrudgingly.

"Do you like popcorn? Pizza?"

Stopping, she turned halfway in his direction. "Why do you want to know?"

"They have popcorn and pizza at the drive-in."

"I thought you worked every night."

Spencer grinned. "Every night except Sunday. My cousin Billy pumps Sundays."

"Not interested," she replied. Then, taking a deep breath, she hurried off.

Trying to shut out the awful *aaooaah* noise

of Spencer's horn as it blared out after her, Laurel trotted along. By the time she got home, it was late morning. The sun was high enough above the stand of Norway pines that the beach was out of the shadows. Miles, just back from a morning's game of golf at the nearby Park Falls course, was relaxing with a can of root beer. Golf in the morning. Afternoon at the beach — a typical Hoop Lake summer day. For a moment she wondered what she was doing with a wiggly baby when she might have been skimming a canoe in and out of the cattails on the north shore.

Before she could resolve this question, though, Miles caught sight of her. "Hey, Pokey, where'd you get that funny-looking baby?"

"She's *not*," Laurel protested, surprised to find herself defending the baby.

"Whose is she?"

Laurel's arms were aching. She shifted Doe onto her right hip. Then she answered: "There's this artist — a sculptor, really, who's renting the Harrisons' old cabin. He's asked me to baby-sit."

Miles raised his eyebrows and emptied his can of root beer. Then, in his usual self-assured way, he zeroed in on the problem. "But, Pokey, you don't know a thing about babies!"

"I can learn, can't I?" Laurel asked, jutting her chin forward. "And . . . well, I thought you'd do me a favor."

Laurel lowered herself into a webbed beach chair. She put Doe on the deck between her feet. Nearby was a sandy plastic mug. Doe reached out and grabbed it. She lifted it to her mouth and began to suck on it.

"Cute," Miles said mockingly.

"Miles — don't be that way," Laurel pleaded. "You must help me. You're going to be a doctor. Those books of yours — some of them must tell about babies."

Miles laughed. "What books? Mine are about dissecting pigs and about organic chemistry. You have to go to the library for the kind of baby books you need. Besides, this is your vacation. So, take the baby back where she came from."

"No," Laurel said, trying to brush sand off the mug and off Doe's face.

"Look, what do you know about this little kid? Does she crawl? Can she walk? Does she have any allergies you should know about?"

"No," Laurel answered.

"No — what?"

Laurel threw her hands up in the air. "I don't know any of those things."

"Laurel, you're hopeless. How do you do it? Are you ever going to grow up and be more practical instead of getting in over your head? How old are you — thirteen?"

"I'm nearly fourteen," she reminded him. "I'll be fourteen in August." But she felt discouraged. Miles sounded like her father or her mother. Especially her mother — tuned out and then — at the wrong time — tuned-in, fault-finding. And she was, as always, Pokey . . . the baby.

Laurel was ready to give up when help came from an unexpected source. Doe looked at Miles. She held the cup out in his direction. "Be-be-be," she said soberly.

Miles grinned. He took the cup. He gave it back. Laurel watched him; she watched Doe. Doe's eyes, Laurel noticed for the first time, were pale, almost colorless, but huge. "Please, Miles, please," Laurel begged.

"The artist and his wife — what kind of people could they be to trust you without asking about your experience? And whatever possessed you to *do* it?"

Laurel slid from the chair. She sat cross-legged in front of Doe. Cautiously she took the cup from the child. Then she tried clapping Doe's hands together as she had seen Ivan do. Doe regarded her suspiciously, but at least she didn't break into tears.

"The wife isn't there," she said. "That's

why Doe's father needs a sitter. Listen, aren't you — all of you — always saying I should learn something new? Besides, this is a job. I'm going to earn money. And maybe Ivan will teach me something about art, too."

"Ivan?"

"Doe's father," Laurel answered, feeling defensive. "He's an art teacher at a college in Minneapolis. Miles, this is important. You're supposed to be looking after me up here, helping me, not picking on me."

"Oh, Laurel. . . ."

Her brother was weakening. "Come on, Miles. Please, *please*!"

"Mmm . . . well, okay, I guess." Miles pulled himself to his feet. "All right, Pokey, if you think you're up to it, if you think you can manage, but. . . ."

"But what?" Laurel challenged.

"A job is a job. If you set out to do this thing," her brother told her in a firm tone, "you must follow through on it, not leave this artist in the lurch. You know, agreeing to care for his child, then losing interest."

"I won't," she promised.

Before Miles could change his mind, Laurel jumped to her feet. "Come on," she urged him. "Let's get started."

He nodded. "Okay — why not? We'll drive

to town. Pick up books at the library. Then we'll stop at the clinic and get some pointers from Jane Collier."

"Jane? Jane's a doctor. You're the one who just told me I need baby books instead of medical stuff." Laurel felt a tug at her foot. She looked down. Doe was untying her shoelace. Laurel bent over and touched the top of the child's head. "Besides, I don't think I should go to the clinic or even to town. Doe's not supposed to be around people or be exposed to germs. And since I haven't asked, I don't think she should be in someone's car, either."

Miles put his hands on his hips. "Good thinking. You are taking this seriously, aren't you?"

Nodding, Laurel lifted Doe into her arms. Miles squinted down at the baby. He made a face. "Hey, what's this black stuff all over her back? What have you done, Pokey?"

Laurel twisted her head for a better look. "Black — what black? Oh, no — ugh — Spencer. He put his hands on her. It's grease from his car."

"Wonderful — terrific." Miles chuckled. "First day on the job and you let the kid get lubed with Pennzoil. That guy Ivan must have a screw loose to trust you. But, yes, I know. You'll study up. Then you'll do everything by the book. Strictly by the book."

Rubbing at Doe's shirt, Laurel sighed. The grease was probably smeared on her, too. As usual, she was incompetent. Miles was treating her as if she were the baby. And he hadn't noticed her new hairdo, either. Well, she'd show him. Show them all. With Ivan and with Doe, things would be different. She'd work her way out of this miserable caterpillar stage. She could do it. She knew she could.

FIVE

Doe rocked back and forth. Laurel watched her intently. So did Ivan. Ivan had abandoned the unfinished sculpture of the woman to begin a carving of a crawling child. The only problem was that Doe didn't crawl. She just got up on her knees and swayed.

"Not enough motion," Ivan commented, bending over his new block of wood. "Not in the clay models I made, either. When will she learn how to shift into forward gear?"

"She'll be harder to watch then," Laurel told him. Her skills and instincts, she thought, were improving. She knew now that Doe could sit and stand even if she couldn't crawl or walk. She knew that the child didn't talk, had no known allergies, and liked to be bounced rather than tickled. Doe slept with a cloth diaper pressed up to her face and her thumb in her mouth. She had five teeth —

with more on the left than on the right so that on the rare occasions when she smiled, she looked like a jack-o'-lantern. She preferred clapping games to songs; and because she explored the world around her by tasting it, everything went into her mouth.

Ivan seemed to be learning about Doe, too. He was as amazed at her as Laurel was. His enthusiasm, though, tapered off when he got involved with chisels and blocks of wood. Then he seemed removed, only half concentrating on the baby. That was where Laurel came in. She had taken over much of the daytime care.

After she read the books from the Park Falls library, she decided she didn't have to tell Ivan that she had never handled a baby before. Child care wasn't too bad, especially when she could contrive to be around Ivan rather than off by herself with Doe. He was easy to be with, accepting, and — best of all — he often talked to Laurel as he worked.

This particular morning, his tone was pensive. "Sometimes I worry, wonder why she doesn't crawl yet."

Laurel leaned her head to one side. "She will . . . soon. And she'll walk. Look how she loves to pretend she can walk." As Laurel spoke, she demonstrated by pulling Doe to her feet.

"Hey — don't do that," Ivan said.

"Why not?"

"It's bad to force children. We shouldn't worry about the crawling, either. She'll do that when she's ready — just like she'll talk when she's ready."

Laurel let Doe drop down lightly on her bottom. She was trying to think what her books said on the subject. She wasn't sure, but she didn't want to argue with Ivan.

He was working rapidly now, chipping away a whole section of wood. "As soon as I take this corner chunk off," he explained, striking a large, blunt-edged chisel with his mallet, "I can outline the haunches. Make them begin to resemble the clay model. Can you see what I mean?"

"Umm . . ." Laurel responded. Usually she was outspoken, but around Ivan she was quieter, afraid of sounding childish or silly.

Ivan didn't seem to be concerned about her silence. "I'm not sure the wood is dry enough," he mused. "It will crack if it's not. But I can fix it. I save the chips — even the sawdust — so I can fill in the cracks and make them invisible. It's one of the tricks of the trade."

Laurel turned from Ivan to Doe, who was chewing on the buckle of her overalls. When Laurel eased it from her mouth, she began to examine the wrinkles in the palms of her hands.

"Someday, Laurel, if you're interested, I'll let you try to carve something. Would you like that, huh?"

"Sure," she answered, looking at his tools scattered over the table, the tree stump, the ground. She leaned forward and picked one up. "Are they all chisels?"

"Sort of," he replied, taking a moment to glance in her direction. "Gouges, to be more precise. Different shapes, different sizes, of course, but they're gouges. Nice, aren't they? Beautiful." Without waiting for her answer, he went on: "It's perfect here at the lake, you know. Something out of my dreams — a new sculpture, peace, Doe . . . and you, of course. Nothing but vibrant promise. Nothing spoiled or skewed or out of place. That's what I love — the dream, the Platonic ideal — forms and lives yet to be shaped. Instead of feeling hounded or pressed against a wall, I feel on the brink of a new life. It's liberating, you know. At moments like this, I feel like Pygmalion. . . ."

Laurel didn't answer. All she understood was that Ivan sounded happy. That he felt his life at Hoop Lake was perfect and that she was, in some way, a part of that perfection.

As Laurel sat waiting for Ivan to speak again, she glanced at Doe. The baby sucked on one finger as she examined the activity around an anthill. After a moment, Laurel shifted her gaze so she was looking at the lake. Miles was trolling out near the sandbar, cruising along the stretch the fishermen called "Easy Street." Down at the Harrisons' dock, Spencer tinkered with the motor on the old rowboat. Across the lake, someone was flying a multicolored kite.

Closer to shore, two nuns, on their bicycle boat, floated along. Watching made Laurel think about her own summer. She wasn't reading anything but baby books, wasn't doing much swimming. It wasn't that she cared, but Miles did. He thought that she was wasting her time. And he was, she knew, going to report this to Jessica, to her parents. No matter what she did, she couldn't please them.

"You're frowning," Ivan said suddenly. "What's up? You must miss all the usual stuff, I guess. Hanging out here can't be very exciting for you."

Laurel opened her mouth to protest. Then she shut it again. Ivan was sensitive. He seemed to understand things. After a moment, she found her voice. "No, it's not just that. More complicated. Family stuff."

"Yeah, yeah — don't tell me. Let me guess. You want a divorce."

"A divorce?"

"Yes, from your family. I felt that way when I was sixteen. . . ."

"I'm not sixteen," Laurel said. She was surprised that Ivan thought she looked older than she was when people usually thought she was younger. "But in August I'll be fourteen."

"August what?"

"Fifteenth," she told him.

"The fifteenth? The day before Allison's birthday. A month before Doe's. Well, it's not important, anyway. Age is of no particular importance. So what were we talking about? Oh, yes — families. Well, when I was fourteen or sixteen, whatever I did wasn't quite right. And then with Allison it was the same thing."

Laurel nodded. Ivan knew how she felt. She wanted to tell him that, but she held back. All she managed was a weak smile.

Ivan reached over and tipped up her chin. "Hey, brooding doesn't help. Come on. I think it's break time. Let's take Doe and go for a swim."

A few minutes later, they were down by

the lake. Laurel had stripped down to the swimsuit she wore under her clothes, Ivan was in his cutoffs, and Doe was naked. First, Ivan hopped in waist-deep water, gently splashing his daughter while Laurel swam. Then they traded places. Laurel took Doe into shallow water and sat down with the baby between her knees. Waves lapped against them. Gold-flecked minnows came close, tickling their toes. Doe stared into the water, stirring it with one thumb. She studied the tiny fish. "Be-be," she said.

After a while, Ivan produced a metal tub and a pile of clothes. "Come on," he urged, calling to Laurel.

Laurel put the baby over one shoulder and struggled to her feet. "What's happening?"

"Wash day," Ivan informed her with his gap-toothed smile.

"What's wrong with driving in to the laundromat?"

"In town?"

Water dripped from her suit. "Yes."

"My truck guzzles gas, and besides, this is more fun. We're roughing it out here in the wilds of Minnesota."

Laurel laughed. Ivan made the simplest things into a game. "Okay, sure. What do we do?"

"Fill the tub."

"I'll do it," Laurel offered eagerly.

Ivan grinned. "Not much of a job. But go ahead. Do it, if you want."

"I do. I will," she said, handing the baby to Ivan. Then she waded out and submerged the tub. Heavy, it sank immediately. Laurel wasn't able to lift it again. She had to use all her strength to drag it back up on shore. "Now what? Do we just throw the clothes in?"

"The clothes? Don't be silly. Where's your pioneer spirit? The tub is for Doe. The clothes we will scrub in the lake, beat them clean against the rocks."

Laurel laughed. "What rocks?" she asked, gesturing at the sandy beach that was strewn with pebbles but nothing that could actually be called a rock.

"Details," Ivan said. "Use your imagination. Now, see — the child sits in a small swimming pool. And we have a whole lake full of fresh water for our wash."

Bending over, Ivan placed Doe in the tub. From the washpile he produced a carrot-stained cotton hat which he perched on top of her head to protect it from burning in the sun. Doe beat against the surface of the water with her fists. Ivan stepped back, looked at her. Then he shook his head.

"What's wrong?" Laurel asked.

"Too deep. If you pick her up for a minute, I'll spill some out."

Laurel did as he had suggested. When she lowered Doe back in the tub, she was sitting in only a few inches of water. She may have been safer, but she looked unhappy. The water didn't splash as well, and there were no minnows in it for her to watch. When Ivan gave her a plastic whale and a tennis ball, she seemed placated. She began trying to feed the ball to the whale.

"Come on," Ivan urged as he gestured toward Laurel. "Let's wash. We'll keep an eye on her. She'll squawk if she needs us."

Ivan produced a tube of biodegradable soap. "Got to protect the environment, too," he said. "Now, look — we squeeze and then we scrub. Unless, of course, you don't want to. Our laundry isn't part of your job, you know."

"Yes . . . but it sounds like fun." It did, but what would her friends at home think if they could see her? She didn't care. This was better than chasing boys in Creve Coeur. Better than hanging out with a creep like Spencer. And, in some way, Laurel felt almost as if she did have a boyfriend. She had Ivan to be with.

SIX

A few minutes later, Ivan and Laurel were washing Levi's and baby clothes, taking part in a relay where he soaped things and she sidestroked to rinse them off. Absorbed, they worked until their feet stirred up so much sand that the water around them turned opaque. Because pieces of laundry kept sinking to the bottom, they had to duck under and hunt for lost items.

While Laurel was wringing out a sweatshirt, suddenly Ivan came from below the water and grabbed her ankles. "Hey! Stop it," she cried, dragging him up by his hair. "No fair. You scared me."

Ivan retrieved the sweatshirt and backed away. He spit water between his teeth and hit her in the eye. "You're too serious," he told her, laughing boyishly. "I'm trying to get you to loosen up, relax."

Grabbing hold of a wet baby blanket from the edge of the dock, she accepted his challenge. "Well, then — take that," she declared as she zapped him over the head and shoulders with it. "And that!"

Ivan dived under water and frog-kicked until he was out of range. "Yes," he said when he came up. "That's more like it. But I hardly felt that at all. I think you need a lot more practice."

Darting after him, Laurel kicked her feet, dragging the blanket behind her. He was fast, however. His arms beat rhythmically against the water as Laurel chased him. Every time she seemed about to close the distance between them, he spurted ahead again.

"I'm going to get you," she threatened. It was almost as if she were chasing Spencer some long-ago summer. Doe was lucky. Doe —

Doe! All of a sudden Laurel forgot about chasing Ivan and turned toward shore. No white hat swayed above the surface of the tub. No little bald head, either. "Ivan," she called. But she was out of breath, and he had gone too far toward the sandbar.

Dropping the blanket, Laurel swam back to shore. As soon as her feet touched bottom, she lunged forward. Awkwardly, she stumbled over the dry sand. She was almost there, but she couldn't see the baby. Where was

Doe? The tub was empty. The only thing floating there was a sunbonnet.

Laurel's eyes darted in all directions. As she saw Ivan racing toward the beach, her heart skidded up and down against the wall of her chest. She was dizzy. Sky, sand, sun, trees, water. Everything spun before her face, reflecting spears of light. Why had she been so careless? And where *was* Doe? Laurel's imagination furnished the unwelcome answer. On the bottom of the lake.

Laurel wailed. She threw her hands up in the air pleading with Ivan to hurry. But just then, something a short distance down the shore caught her eye. In the shade, near a green rowboat, she saw Spencer. He was sitting on the sand and next to him, staring into the water, was a pink-headed baby.

Spencer had taken Doe from the tub. This was his idea of a joke. Speechless with rage, Laurel raced toward him. By now, Ivan was close behind. He overtook her. He spurted forward and grabbed his daughter.

Struggling for breath, he examined the child. When he was satisfied that she was unharmed, he thrust her into Laurel's arms. "Here — she's okay. Hold her."

A moment later, enraged, he began to swear at Spencer. Laurel, not knowing what else to do, fled in the direction of the cabin.

She clutched the baby, murmuring what she hoped were soothing words; but Doe, startled by the commotion, was howling.

Laurel, trying to calm them both, kept talking. The back of her throat felt swollen. As she talked, she began almost automatically to diaper and dress the child. Then she gave her some juice while she sat in the rocking chair shivering, trying not to look over at the half-finished sculpture of the woman. Somehow Laurel knew that the woman was Allison, Doe's mother. Her baby had been in danger, and she hadn't even known it. Besides, Allison wouldn't have left her baby alone.

Finally, Ivan appeared in the doorway. As Laurel looked up at him, her throat swelled even more. Suddenly she began to sob — dry, wrenching sobs with no tears. Ivan moved forward. He took Doe from her arms. Then, balancing the baby on one shoulder, he knelt before the rocker.

"Not your fault, Laurel," he crooned softly, talking to her in the voice he usually reserved for his daughter. "Not yours at all, honey. All mine. I got carried away. So don't cry. She's safe — all right. Look, look at her drooling down my back."

Laurel continued to sob. This was what Miles had anticipated. Everything she touched went wrong. What was she doing? She felt young, lost. She wanted someone to hold her the way Ivan was holding Doe.

Ivan kept talking in the same low tones. Sitting cross-legged on the floor, he tried to soothe her. "There, there — you reacted fast. Perfectly. Your friend was stupid, and he did a stupid thing. But our eyes weren't off the baby for more than a few seconds. You know that. We wouldn't let anything happen to this little girl. We're responsible people. Come on, Laurel dear. Come on, take it easy now."

As he talked, he used one foot to move the rockers on the chair. At last, Laurel's sobs began to subside. Ivan sat beside her patiently, speaking, yet pausing occasionally to nuzzle the baby.

Watching Ivan, Laurel continued to sit there motionlessly. She let Ivan rock the chair and soothe her even when she knew it was no longer necessary. She liked the half-dim cabin with its stacks of tools and clothing and its general air of disarray. It felt like a pioneer cabin. Laurel squinted. It could have been a hundred years ago. A hundred years ago, Doe could have been her baby, Ivan her husband. And the laundry, her laundry. It was an unsettling idea. It made her giggle.

"What?" Ivan asked, surprised at her sudden shift of mood.

She pulled on her braid and felt a thin river of water seep down her back. Though she wanted to tell Ivan what she was imagining, she was embarrassed.

"Come on now," he urged. "What are you laughing at?"

Laurel looked down. Her pioneer vision began to fade and images of the scene at the lake replaced them. Ivan swimming with the clothes. Ivan racing toward Doe. He puzzled her. He was old at one moment, young the next. If she needed to be more responsible, maybe he did, too. Perhaps Spencer had been right to take Doe. And how had it all happened? Because of something as unimportant as the laundry.

"What *are* you thinking about?" Ivan asked. "A moment ago you were laughing. Now you look as if you'd lost your last friend."

Laurel took a deep breath. "I was thinking about the laundry," she said at last. "That it should be done at the coin place in town. If your clothes haven't all sunk to the bottom of the lake. And, Ivan, we mustn't *ever* leave Doe alone in that tub. Never again."

Ivan propped a hand behind himself and struggled to his feet. Doe was, by now, half asleep. Moving slowly, Ivan placed her on her stomach in the crib. He covered her. Then he turned back to Laurel. "You are a treasure — some kind of uncut gem or a piece of golden locust waiting to be shaped," he told her in a light, even tone. "I hope everyone in your family values you as I am learning to."

Then, without another word, he turned and headed out to collect what was left of his clothes.

SEVEN

Laurel listened as the bow of the canoe made a slurping sound when it bobbed over the water lilies. When Ivan stopped paddling, she did, too. Turning, she checked up on Doe. This daylong canoe trip had been Ivan's idea. Laurel was excited to have a chance to be with him when he wasn't working.

It was midmorning, and they were near the west end of Hoop Lake with two more lakes ahead of them. Doe, eyes blinking sleepily, was strapped in the baby carrier. The carrier was lashed to the middle thwart. Above it swayed a lean-to which Ivan had devised to protect her from the sun.

Dragonflies swooped through the air, as if involved in a special mission. A turtle plopped off a half-submerged log and swam away. A flock of mallards cruised near shore. Frogs sprang from one glossy leaf to another.

The sun made her skin prickle. On shore aspens and birches whispered to one another, their leaves shining like silver coins. Laurel stretched. She felt a sense of timelessness, of weightlessness. She lowered her arms until they were extended sideways, then moved them up and down slowly, wondering if she could rise up from the water and hover overhead, surveying the world around them.

"Poised for lift-off?" Ivan asked, as if wanting to fly was a quite understandable idea.

"Yes," she agreed.

"Do you know why you feel so good?"

"Why?" she asked, lowering her arms and hugging them to her chest.

"Because this moment is perfect. It's one of those times when we just exist and being alive seems simple because the dragon isn't breathing fire."

Laurel giggled self-consciously. She shifted sideways so she could glance at Ivan, who was bent forward playing a finger game with Doe. "What dragon?" she asked.

"Time," he answered. "It's the dragon that captures us, makes us afraid of today, tomorrow, and the day after that."

"Afraid?"

"Yes, like I think you are sometimes. But I'm more afraid, because I have more to be afraid of. It was easy when it was just worrying about my folks and whether people liked me. I used to worry about feeling lonely. Now I see that whatever we do, we are always alone. . . ."

Alone — even when he had been with Allison? Alone when he was with Doe? Laurel didn't like the idea that a person could be married, be a parent, and still feel alone. Especially not today when she felt safe — as if she'd never be lonely again. She shivered. She watched a water bug skate between the lily pads. "Do you miss Allison?"

"No," he said, "no . . . not after a while. Being a parent changed her, leeched out her sense of fun and adventure. Then she started to worry all the time, complaining and imagining things."

"Mmm . . ." Laurel murmured, anxious to indicate that she sympathized with him.

"It's hard, though," Ivan continued, "not having someone else around the clock. I never knew how much pressure was involved in looking after Doe. That's why it's been great these last two weeks. You've been a lifesaver."

Flattered yet timid, Laurel didn't reply. She felt close to Ivan. She liked drifting among the lily pads, listening to him. It was almost as if the two of them were acting out a scene in a movie.

For a few moments, they bobbed in silence. Then Ivan spoke again. "It's Doe who makes me feel afraid," he confided. "I'm always wondering if I'm doing the right thing and she's all right."

"Look at her. Of course she's all right."

Ivan shrugged. "It's just that she's so serious, quiet. . . . Maybe we don't talk to her enough."

"Well, then, let's talk more and see what happens," Laurel suggested.

Ivan brightened. "It might make a difference. It is worth a try, isn't it?"

"I think so. . . ."

Suddenly Ivan looked uneasy. "Am I boring you? Am I yakking too much about Doe and bringing up stuff too heavy for a summer day?"

"No, of course not," she insisted.

"Then speak up. Tell me what's going on in that head of yours."

She scratched her back just above the strap of her halter. A frog dived from a lily pad into the lake. Rings of water rolled out, spreading wider and wider. "I think . . ." she answered, groping for something appropriate to say, "that it might be nice to be a frog."

Ivan chuckled. "So you think we'd be happy if we could be transformed into frogs?"

Laurel leaned over the bow of the boat and

trailed her fingers in the water, touched the waxy petals of a lily. Without knowing how, she'd managed to say the right thing. "Sure, why not?"

"It's a frog's life, huh?"

Laurel laughed. "Isn't that what we were talking about? Out in the sun. Look how easy, how lazy. . . ."

Ivan didn't answer immediately. When he did, his voice had a hard edge to it. "Don't you bet on it. Sometimes dreamers like us see only what they wish to see, Laurel. Why, those frogs you envy are perfectly safe — except, of course, for being preyed on by turtles, gulls, ducks, fish. Life has a way of devouring us, dumping us still kicking into the dark belly of a whale, without considering if we have the faith, and the innocence, of a Jonah."

Laurel shuddered.

"Sorry," Ivan said. "I didn't mean to throw a cloud over the day. I forgot myself. And why are we dawdling? We should get going. Come on. And how about a song to entertain our passenger?"

So, singing "Mary Had a Little Lamb," they picked up their paddles and nosed the canoe into the channel between Hoop Lake and Fishhook. As soon as they edged out of the water lilies, the current began to pull them forward.

"What's it like through here?" Ivan asked.

Laurel thought for a moment. She'd made the trip with her family many times, but they'd always come by motorboat instead of canoe.

"Fast," she answered. "But not too bad."

"Is it safe enough for the baby? There's no danger of tipping?" Ivan asked.

"Oh, no," she assured him. "It's mostly waves."

"Then we'll be fine," he said. "Let's go for it."

Working together, the two of them maneuvered the canoe through the channel. They scraped against a few rocks, got wedged momentarily on a submerged log, then floated through. Doe made some small clucking noises, as if she was trying to say that riding in choppy water was fun.

"Like an amusement park, Doe-baby. Nice, so nice. Easy does it."

As the canoe came out of the channel into Fishhook Lake, Laurel looked back. Ivan was a good canoeist. Appreciative, she offered him a piece of information. "Hoop Lake is shaped like a fishhook — and Fishhook like a hoop."

He laughed. "I feel lik- I'm being given the guided tour. And I love it. So where, my sweet guide, do we go from here?"

Laurel gestured with her paddle. "The outlet to Island Lake is across there — where the cattails are."

"There?" Ivan asked, pivoting the canoe toward the center of the lake.

"Yes . . . but no," she told him. She swayed in her seat. She liked Ivan calling her his sweet guide, but it was a responsibility she took seriously. She turned sideways. "You ought to stay near the shore. The waves are rough when a wind blows up."

Ivan didn't change direction. "Don't worry. There's no wind and not a cloud in the sky. Trust me."

Instead of arguing, Laurel nodded. Then, stroking in silence, she watched as he steered straight toward Island Lake, changing course only if a motorboat seemed to be swerving too close to them.

Halfway across, Doe began to squirm and fuss. Ivan distracted her with a raw carrot from his knapsack. "She'll chew on that for a while," he said, "but we'll have our hands full later. So let's pick up the pace. Besides, there's a boat back there that seems to be following us. We haven't done anything, have we? Do the police have a water patrol around here — like up at the border?"

Laurel shook her head. "Of course not!" The idea of the fat, lazy Park Falls policemen checking up on boaters was ridiculous. She wasn't disturbed by the sound of a motorboat, a common Minnesota noise.

Ivan, however, seemed to like pretending that they were being followed. "Stroke," he urged. "Stroke," he repeated as they paddled the canoe through the short inlet into Island Lake.

Doe had thrown the carrot aside and begun to whimper. But instead of stopping to placate her, they paddled until they had slipped around to the far shore of the small island. There, at a sandy point, they beached the boat. Then Ivan jumped from the stern into knee-deep water.

"Get out," he told Laurel as he unbuckled Doe. "Hustle onto shore. I want to pull the boat up. Here, take the baby and duck behind those bushes."

Was this another game? Laurel was confused. She looked around. "Be careful of the poison ivy," she warned. "It's everywhere."

"Keep your voice down," Ivan whispered.

A moment later, she and Ivan were crouched with Doe behind some blueberry bushes.

"Don't move," he said.

The drone of the motor got louder as the boat approached. Laurel rocked Doe to keep her from crying. Though she wanted to tell Ivan that he was being silly, her voice stuck in her throat. Maybe they were in some kind of danger.

At last, when Laurel thought she could stand it no longer, the prow of a boat edged around the island and floated into sight. It was a green rowboat with a fishing motor on the back. It was trolling slowly as if it was looking for someone or something. There was only one passenger.

Suddenly Ivan rolled backward onto the grass. He started to laugh. "It's your boy-friend, Laurel. The Harrison boy. He's a dreadful nuisance, you know. Someone should teach him a lesson."

"He's a geek," Laurel said. "And he's *not* my boyfriend."

"Are all boys geeks?" Ivan asked.

"The ones I know. Or else I'm one, and that's why they don't like me."

"But what about this one?" Ivan asked, removing a pebble from Doe's hand. "Is he worse? The essence of geekdom?"

"Yes," she said, nodding enthusiastically.

"Well, then, let's invite him to join us for lunch."

Laurel rolled onto her stomach and reached out to chuck Doe under the chin. "Why?"

"Why not? We'll wine and dine him, so to speak. Then take the painter from the canoe and rope him to a sapling. We'll give him a day or two to meditate on his sins."

Laurel smiled uneasily at the image of Spencer left on the island tied to a tree.

"You're grinning, honey, but you don't think I'm funny."

Her scalp prickled. Ivan seemed able to see into her head. "Mmm ... no. ... Besides, isn't it time for lunch?"

Nodding agreeably, Ivan winked at her. Then he winked at Doe. "Sure. I got carried away. So forget what I said and let's have lunch. Our little girl is hungry, too. Aren't you, noodle?"

EIGHT

Laurel expected Spencer to go away, but he didn't. Instead, he moved farther from shore; and dropping anchor, he began to fish. Laurel was irritated at his nosiness, but she didn't know what she could do about it.

The best thing, she decided, was to ignore him. First, she and Ivan fed Doe. Then they had peanut-butter sandwiches and Kool-Aid. After a while, using the bottom of the canoe for a crib, Ivan put Doe down for a nap.

"You want to pick blueberries?" Ivan asked.

Laurel shook her head lazily. "They're still green."

"Shall we explore, then?"

"Not me," she told him. "I'll stay here. Someone should. . . ."

"You're right. Okay. Well . . . I won't be long. I'll be back soon," he promised.

As he wandered off, Laurel lay on the shore watching cumulus clouds drift overhead. She wanted to think about Ivan, yet it was hard to concentrate when Spencer was floating nearby. She sat up and stared out at the lake.

Spencer's back was turned as if he was oblivious to her presence. After a long while, without glancing in her direction, he stowed his pole, pulled up anchor, and disappeared. Laurel wondered what time it was. It seemed as if Ivan had been gone for a long time. Squinting, she tried to see if she could guess the time by locating the sun. Because the sun was half covered by cloud, she couldn't.

The air was getting cooler. Laurel went over to check on Doe. She looked into the bottom of the canoe. The child stirred. Her skin was red, and she felt warm to the touch — no, not warm, hot. Laurel stood up. "Ivan," she called.

The baby jerked convulsively. Bending down, Laurel scooped Doe up in her arms. "Ivan," she called again. "Ivan!"

There was no answer. Laurel looked from side to side. She turned toward the wooded center of the small island. He should have answered immediately. Trying to decide what to do, she looked down as Doe pulled lethargically at her braid. Then she peered back into the trees. "I-van? I-van?"

As she was shouting, someone grabbed her from behind. "Got you both!" a voice barked in her ear.

For a moment she struggled, trying to control her panic. Then suddenly she twisted far enough around to catch sight of her captor. It was Ivan. While she faced in the other direction, he'd waded from the lake and crept up behind her.

"Let go," she demanded.

He released her immediately. "Look, I goofed. I've really scared you. I'm sorry. Really, I am. It was meant to be a joke."

"How could you do that?" she cried. "There's nothing funny about this at all. Nothing!"

"Hey, wait a minute. What's up? What's wrong?"

Laurel stepped back and looked down at the overheated baby nestled in her arms. "The baby's sick. She's red, and she's hot."

Ivan took Doe immediately. He put her down on the ground and stripped off her clothes. Then the problem was apparent. Sunburn. Despite their precautions, she had been burned by the rays reflecting off the water.

"I'm so stupid," Ivan said. "The sun is strong — even in the shade. I should have known. We've got to get back."

A short while later, hastily packed up, they launched the canoe and headed east as Doe lay apathetically in the carrier. She seemed too tired to cry.

Laurel looked back over her shoulder. "When we get home we can call Jane Collier and ask. Jane's Spencer's cousin, and she's one of the doctors at the clinic."

"I don't think so," Ivan said. "I know what I need for sunburn. I can handle it. But still, no matter how carefully I watch Doe, something seems to go wrong."

"No, that's not true. You do a great job with her," Laurel insisted, raising her voice so Ivan could hear her over the rising afternoon wind.

"Dangerous," he muttered. "Like the lily-pad marsh."

Trying to understand him, Laurel bent harder over the paddle. Their progress was slow because of waves that had begun to blow up while they were on the island. By the time they were back on the large round surface of Fishhook Lake, whitecaps tipped the waves and the sun had disappeared behind clouds that were rolling in from the west.

Doe was damp with perspiration. Ivan dried her face with a cloth. Then he pointed the canoe toward the channel to Hoop Lake.

Laurel didn't like what was happening. The wind was coming from behind them, and the waves were too large for a canoe.

Unruffled, Ivan nudged the boat skillfully. "Okay, okay now — press on," he urged. He was talking both to Laurel and to himself. As he paddled, he kept talking. "That's it, honey. Yes, pull evenly. Yes, yes, the waves are pushing us. They're helping us, and they're nice, friendly waves, too. See. . . ."

The canoe bobbed and rocked. Water slapped against it, splashed over the gunwales. The muscles in Laurel's arms and shoulders felt leaden, but she didn't dare relax. The adventure Ivan had looked for all day seemed to have come upon them, but it was not the kind of lighthearted one he might have anticipated. Laurel continued to lift her paddle and pull it through the water. She tried not to think about what she would be doing if she were at home. She and Miles would be in the living room doing a jigsaw puzzle, lounging about watching the storm blow in.

All of a sudden Laurel realized that Miles didn't know where she was. She hadn't told him about this trip. If something happened, he wouldn't have any idea where she was or why she was missing. Families needed to know things like that. Laurel shuddered.

Families should know — not only her family, but Doe's, too. Allison didn't know that her baby was out on a dangerous lake. If something happened, how would she find out?

The wind increased, and drops of rain began to pelt down on them. Ivan paused to adjust the angle of the lean-to so Doe would be more sheltered. As he did this, the canoe — pivoted by a wave — lurched. Laurel lunged with her paddle, trying to correct their angle. If the waves hit them broadside, the canoe would tip. Laurel's mind raced. She and Ivan could cling to the boat and drift with it. But Doe couldn't.

With a powerful sweep, Ivan brought the boat back on its course. "Easy, girl, easy," he said, crooning loud enough to be heard over the wind and the splatting sound of the rain. "It's going to be fine. Yes, that's it. Feather the paddle. Or recover underwater, but watch for the wind. Yes, steady now. A sunburn is just sunburn and a wave is no more than a hill of water with a white ruff on it. So, trust me. Yes, that's it."

Ivan's voice soothed her. Later, as she had hot chocolate with Miles, she could laugh about her adventure. Well, not really. Her brother would be unhappy that Laurel had gone off on a canoe trip without telling him.

But they were going to make it. Once the channel had been negotiated, they'd be back onto Hoop Lake. From the marsh to the cabin was a short distance, and they could get there paddling in and out of coves.

By the time they edged into the channel, needles of icy rain were pricking Laurel's shoulders. Still, the worst was behind them. They had not tipped in the middle of the lake. Soon they'd be safe. As Laurel stroked, she thought about safety. About safety and babies and water. Babies and washtubs. Unspoken questions throbbed in her head. The bottom of the lake, the bottom of the tub. What difference did any of it make if a baby could drown in a few inches of water? Canoes were delicate, dangerous boats. How could anyone protect a baby if the boat swamped?

"Pull for the channel," Ivan urged. "As soon as we make it there, we're home free. Look — the rain's blowing over, and Doe is looking better now that it's cooled off. Besides, babies are tougher than the rest of us, I sometimes think."

Laurel listened to Ivan, yet something that she hadn't considered began to nag at her. Something about the channel. Then as they swung around the cattails into its mouth, she remembered. The channel flowed in the other direction. With a motor it didn't matter, but they couldn't paddle upstream in a canoe. And it was too deep to wade. Yes, they could portage. But how — especially in the rain — would they manage a portage with a sick baby?

Laurel blamed herself, too. She knew about the channel and canoes. Why hadn't she warned Ivan hours ago? Because she hadn't remembered. Suddenly she heard her mother's voice — sensible, critical — telling her that she was careless and immature. She was afraid — too tired to think, too tired to cope.

Just then, however, something attracted her attention. Tethered at the edge of the channel was a green rowboat. It had an outboard motor clamped to the back. Sitting in it, hunched in an old poncho, was Spencer.

Ivan assessed the situation quickly. They needed help. Spencer, with his motor, was in a position to give it. Without hesitation, Ivan steered the canoe alongside the rowboat. Nodding brusquely, Spencer leaned out and caught the bow. He was only a few inches from Laurel. "Give me your painter," he told her. "The rope — right. I'll tie it on and tow you."

Ivan accepted the rescue as though he'd planned it. Leaning forward, he picked up Doe and cradled her in his arms. "Fate," he told Laurel as the gasoline motor dragged them upstream, "has once again intervened for the better. Charon is ferrying us back from the Underworld. I was pretty good today. But you were magnificent, Laurel. Magnificent. Grace under pressure — and more so."

Laurel's fingers and toes tingled. She didn't think she had been magnificent. Things had gone wrong. So many of them. And yet listening to Ivan made her want to forget almost everything.

NINE

JULY

July had arrived. Laurel was elbow-deep in soap suds as she did her best to create order in Ivan's kitchen. Because it was a combination kitchen and bathroom, he referred to it as the "bitchen." The word also indicated his attitude when he had to work there.

In the three weeks that Laurel had been baby-sitting for Doe, the kitchen had gotten worse. Now when she came in the morning, it was piled with damp towels, dirty clothes, food-encrusted dishes. The linoleum floor was gritty with sand, stenciled with muddy footprints. For a while Laurel had ignored its condition, but gradually she had begun to tackle it.

"Why are you doing this housekeeping stuff?" Ivan kept asking her. "It's not part of your job. You're here to keep Doe company — and me. Just leave the mess, and I'll get to it in the evenings . . . when I'm alone. . . ."

She wasn't working hard just because of the money Ivan paid her each Friday. Every smile and casual "Thanks, honey" from Ivan encouraged her to redouble her efforts. She had seemed to be making progress, too, until the day Doe started to crawl. Then kitchen work became more of a problem.

This particular morning, Laurel solved it by dragging Ivan's footlocker across the doorway so the baby couldn't escape. Once she had moved everything sharp out of reach, the kitchen was a relatively safe place. Safe but messy. Laurel sighed.

Everywhere she looked she saw sticky bowls, spoons, and congealing trails of yellow batter that Ivan had abandoned after trying to make pancakes. Now while she wrestled with the dishes, he was outside chipping at a new sculpture — a carving of his own bearded head. When she looked out, she saw him reflected in the mirror he'd propped on the stump.

Then, turning away from the window, she flipped a dishtowel over Doe's head. "Peek-a-boo," she called.

"Be-be-be," Doe said, as she pulled herself up next to the stove.

"Yes, I see you."

Doe balanced herself precariously on her

feet. She reached above her head. "Ba-ba-ba."

"No . . . no," Laurel told her. "Stay away from the burners. Hot. Listen — the stove is *hot!*"

When Doe didn't respond to the urgent tone of her voice, Laurel leaped forward and moved her away. "Stoves are not for little girls. I am trying to spend more time talking to you, but you don't listen to me. No! Now here — roll the ball. Good girl. Yes."

Laurel's progress was slow because Doe crawled after her like a puppy, tugging at her ankles, whining for attention. According to Ivan, Doe was crabby because she was teething.

"Okay, okay," Laurel told her, wiping her hands and looking around for something to amuse the child.

Laurel reached out. She picked up a pot and an aluminum bowl. She gave them to Doe. Then she took a metal spoon from the dishrack and clanged it against the bowl. She drummed it against the pot, harder this time. Doe crawled over to take a look.

Her gray eyes widened. She blinked with surprise as the sound reverberated around her. After a few moments, her mouth curved into one of its rare jack-o'-lantern smiles. She took the spoon from Laurel and banged it herself.

Laurel squatted. She watched as Doe continued to beat and blink. The baby was unusually animated. She even seemed interested in whether Laurel liked the noise, too.

"Good girl," Laurel told her. "You are a good girl, and I like you more than I used to. Do you like me? Do you?"

For a moment, Doe gazed at Laurel. Then she began to pound again.

"Yes, you are good, little one. But why do you always want your daddy instead of me? I'm good to you, aren't I? So how come, huh?"

Before she could finish, a voice cut in, interrupting her. "What's going on in here?"

Ivan, a mallet and a gouge in one hand, had come to check on them. Grinning, he bounded over the footlocker and landed beside Laurel.

"Well, look at my daughter," he said, seating himself next to her. "Nothing wrong with her. She loves this racket. And what a sense of rhythm. Listen to her."

Ivan put down his gouge. "You're some baby," he said. Then he took his mallet and thumped it against the bowl.

"Be-be-be!" Doe shrieked.

She was willing to accept Ivan's participation, but when Laurel attempted to bang along with her, she grabbed possessively for the second spoon.

"Hey," Ivan told her. "You must share. Now look, we all play. We're going to make a whole symphony. Yes, Laurel. But don't be so tentative. She's going to become a little dictator if we never argue with her. Yes, that's it. Ivan and his all-girl orchestra. Wonderful!"

Laurel laughed. This was better than cleaning the kitchen. Content, she watched as Doe threw down the spoon and reached for the gouge. Doe cocked her head to one side and tapped the tool against a pot.

Lunging forward, Laurel pried it out of Doe's fingers. "Sharp," she told the child. "No. That's not for you. Use the spoon. Here."

Doe turned to her father. Opening her mouth wide, she began to wail.

Ivan frowned. "I hate when we have to do that. We're interfering with her natural curiosity. Why doesn't she experiment with things that aren't sharp or dangerous?"

"Because they're not as interesting." Laurel chuckled as she rocked back on her heels. "Can't we give her a spatula? She's crying, but I don't see any tears."

Ivan looked at Laurel. He nodded. "Right, my friend. A spatula is both safe and appropriate. Now, Doe-baby, here. Let's get on with it. How about a rendition of 'Stars and Stripes Forever'?"

Ivan kissed his daughter on top of her head. He put the spoon back into her hand. Then he began to wave his arms like a conductor. He hummed noisily as Laurel and Doe beat on their instruments. After another minute or two, he turned and patted Laurel on the shoulder. "Just look at Doe. She's so full of life. I'm proud of you, honey."

As Ivan spoke, he patted her shoulder once again. Laurel flushed with pleasure. His touch was reassuring. It was comfortable, comforting. Or it would be if she could get used to it. Now, even though she liked it, she knew she stiffened slightly, almost as if she had been burned.

Embarrassed, she scrambled to her feet. "I've got to get this place straightened up," she declared, plunging her hands back into the dishwater.

Ivan took hold of his tools and stood up. "It looks terrific to me," he said. "Why bother? Why don't we all go for a walk or climb a tree? Or we could fly kites."

"Oh, Ivan, we can't — there's so much to do."

Ivan laughed. "That's you, Laurel. Your notion. I never asked you to do this stuff. Not that it's not nice, of course. You are a whiz."

In her haste to prove him correct, Laurel swished a plate through the water. As she flung it into the dishrack, she chipped it against the edge of the sink. "Oh, no," she groaned. "I'm so clumsy."

"Not to worry," Ivan said. "It's no big deal. Rule number one about life: Don't sweat the small things. Rule number two: They're all small things."

"Really?" she asked. She moved a step closer to him, waiting for more philosophizing or another touch of his hand.

But she didn't get either, because Ivan was looking off into the distance. "Say, Laurel, can you cook, too? I'm all thumbs in here. If I hung around in the kitchen, could you — maybe — teach me just a few simple things?"

Laurel brushed a piece of lint from her shirt. She didn't know how to cook, but she wasn't inclined to admit that to Ivan. "Well . . ." she said hesitantly.

Ivan reached down and picked up Doe. "If it's a problem, forget it," he said. "It was just a suggestion."

"No, wait," Laurel said, "I can help out. Even buy the food when I'm in town. Just tell me what you like. Okay?"

Hugging the baby, Ivan flashed a smile in Laurel's direction. "Are you sure?"

She nodded. "I'm sure."

"Great. Wonderful. Don't worry about what I like or anything. Be adventurous. I'll just learn from you. Look, I can keep Doe in the pen and give her lunch. Then I'll give you grocery money, and you can go when you want instead of waiting for her to take her nap."

A short while later, as Laurel pedaled her bike up the road from the cabin, she tried to imagine what she was going to cook for dinner. How could she teach Ivan? She only knew how to make two things in the kitchen: scrambled eggs and popcorn.

But she did have an idea. Her first stop in town would be the library. If she had learned to care for Doe from a book, then she could learn to cook the same way. "If I can read, I can cook," she told herself as she skimmed past the Harrison house.

Because she was absorbed in her thoughts, she didn't spot Spencer until it was too late. "Wait," he called, stepping out from behind the garage. He thrust himself into her path and caught hold of her handlebars. "How's the baby? Does that guy really know how to take care of a kid?"

"Sexist," Laurel said in her most scathing tone of voice. "Let go of me."

"Does he? Sometimes I wonder."

"Of course he does. Everybody makes a few

mistakes, you know. Now take your hands away, will you? You're going to get everything all greasy again."

"Baby's kind of cute, you know."

Laurel wanted to agree with him, but she didn't let herself. "Get out of my way."

"How about the drive-in?"

"No!"

"Not you, silly. The baby. Then you can be alone with Ivan the hunk."

Laurel glared at Spencer. "Pervert," she said. Then shifting her weight, she kicked him in the shin.

TEN

Once Laurel had escaped from Spencer, she cycled along feeling good. As she went past the gas station, she waved to Annie Harrison. A short while later, she waved at a group of nuns as they walked along in their cotton shirts and shorts. Before they had moved in at the peeled-bark lodge, she had assumed that all nuns wore black, shaved their heads, and talked only about religion, but these nuns were young teachers on vacation. They didn't look serious and wear their habits on any day except Sunday. Most of the time, they chatted and giggled among themselves, reminding Laurel of how she acted when she was around her classmates. But all that silliness, she reminded herself, had been before she met Ivan and Doe.

Preoccupied, she pulled up in front of the library. Soon, having consulted the card catalogue, she was poring over the *Joy of Cooking*. As she leaned against the bookshelves thumbing through chicken dishes, a voice startled her.

"Hello, stranger."

Laurel wheeled around. She dropped her book. It was Miles. "Oh, hi," she said.

"What's up, Pokey."

"Well — uh — oh, nothing much."

Miles bent down and retrieved the book. "Since when do you cook?"

"Since today," Laurel admitted self-consciously.

He grinned. "So why didn't you ask me for lessons? And what are we going to have for dinner?"

Laurel tugged at her braid. "Well, you see, it's not for us. It's for Ivan."

"For Ivan?" her brother asked, raising his eyebrows. "Why is everything for Ivan? I'm thinking that I ought to check out this Ivan character before Jessie comes. Annie told me he's a good, responsible father. But still . . . Mom and Dad — "

"Oh, Miles. . . ." Laurel had known trouble was coming. Now it was here.

Miles took hold of her elbow and edged her toward the door where their voices wouldn't disturb the librarian and the other patrons of the Park Falls library. "You're getting too independent, miss. Besides, I think this Ivan is taking advantage of you. I've hardly seen you. And when Jessie comes, you'll be too busy baby-sitting to see her, either."

Laurel sat down on the wooden umbrella rack. This was going to be a long, unpleasant conversation. "No, no. I'll see Jessie."

"I don't believe you."

"Get off my back," Laurel said. "You're always telling me to grow up, be on my own, aren't you?"

Miles nodded, but he looked skeptical. "Isn't your behavior pattern going to change sometime? Isn't — "

"I don't want to talk about this," Laurel said, only half aware that her voice was getting louder. "Stop jumping on me, accusing me. Okay, okay, I'm not as good as Jessica, not as good as you. So what else is new?"

"Pokey!"

"Can't you call me Laurel?"

"Yes, *Laurel*, but stop trying to distract me. If you don't like the nickname, that's understandable. We'll discuss that some other time. But right now, we're discussing what you're doing with your summer. First, you've taken on a baby, and now it's cooking. I think you're getting out of your depth. Into some kind of fantasy world."

Laurel jumped to her feet. "Leave me alone," she said. "I'm tired of all this. In our family everything is an intellectual discussion or psychology lesson. I'm tired of it. I'm *so* tired of it. Why don't we just *do* things, just *feel* things? Why don't we? Why?"

"Keep your voice down," Miles muttered. "We don't have to broadcast this to the whole town. But look at you, you're nearly hysterical over a cookbook. I'm worried, Pokey. I eally am. I'm going to have a talk with Jessie. Maybe we should call Mom."

Laurel clutched the cookbook to her chest. She was not winning this battle. She had to -dopt some other method. If her brother in- 'isted on calling her mother, there would be trouble. Her mother could tune out for only so long; but when she, even belatedly and from Sri Lanka, paid attention, Laurel could expect a series of unwelcome orders. And the first one would be: Don't see Ivan or Doe anymore. Just when Doe was beginning to warm up to her, just when she was getting to know Ivan.

She swallowed hard. "Oh, Miles," she pleaded, trying to keep a whiny tone from creeping into her voice, "I'm sorry. Really I am. I'll try to be better, spend more time with you. We'll finish the puzzle. I'll play chess if you wish."

"Trouble," Miles said. "In one way or another you're always trouble."

"Don't say that. Please give me a chance," Laurel begged.

"Why?"

"Because I'm asking you. Please, Miles, please."

Miles frowned. "Yeah, right. Same tactics you always use. And I, all of us, give in because it's easier than dealing with you. Okay. So check out your book, and I'll give you a lift home."

"I've got my bike," Laurel said, careful to avoid mentioning that she had to shop for groceries or that she didn't intend to come home yet.

Miles nodded, but he didn't look satisfied. "All right, then. But be home by six. And if things don't improve, I *am* going to call Mom."

Laurel blinked hard as she tried to keep tears from welling up in her eyes. If she had to be home by six, that meant she couldn't stay to sample the dinner she and Ivan were going to cook. She pressed her lips together. Nothing she said at this point would be any help. Ivan treated her as an adult. When would her family stop acting as if she were a baby? "I'll be home," she agreed.

"See you at six. And don't be late now. I

mean it. I want to feel I can trust you."

As Miles turned and headed down the library steps toward the car, Laurel looked after him angrily. "Grinch," she whispered. "Sometimes I hate you. I really do!"

Her mood had not improved by the time she got back to the cabin. She didn't know whether she had smoothed things over with Miles. He might still cause problems for her. Besides, the closer she got toward helping Ivan do something with the naked, pimpled chicken on the counter before her, the more anxious she felt.

Doe was napping. Ivan, absorbed, tapped away on the crawling baby. The self-portrait had been pushed aside so that he could shape the bottoms of the baby's feet.

Laurel read through the directions. She didn't know what "baste" meant. She'd always thought that was a sewing word. Cookbooks didn't seem to say what they meant — at least not the one she'd checked out.

With a growl, she slammed the book closed. Turning, she was surprised to find Ivan standing in the doorway behind her. "Laurel," he said, speaking softly so he wouldn't wake Doe. "Someone's here to see you."

Laurel grimaced. The only person that could be was Spencer. And she was certain she didn't want to see him. Cradling the chicken in her arms, she stomped out the door.

But it wasn't Spencer. It was Miles. Well, let him check, she told herself. What had he found? Nothing very surprising. A sleeping baby, his sister with a chicken, and Ivan sculpting.

"My brother," she explained to Ivan. "Ivan — Miles."

The two shook hands. Miles was younger, of course. Although he was taller than Ivan, he had no beard and his face had a soft, youngish look.

"Nice," Miles said, gesturing toward the half-finished carvings sitting in the yard. "But tell me, how do you work on so many things at once?"

Ivan, who had seemed concerned when the stranger was unidentified, relaxed. "Don't know," he admitted. "Think it's one of my failings. This taking things up and putting them aside."

"Why? Isn't that the creative spirit at work?" Miles asked, speaking as if he were a longtime friend of Ivan's. "I don't know a lot about art, but these things look good to me."

"Thanks," Ivan said.

Miles stuffed his hands in his pockets. "Say, what do you do up here when you're not carving? Do you get any exercise? If I weren't leaving, I'd ask if you wanted to play golf."

Ivan smiled. "I don't play," he said, "so you've gotten off lucky. Besides, because of the baby, I have so little time. Even with Laurel around doing a super job."

Something in Ivan's voice made Laurel wince. Suddenly her brother and Ivan were buddies; and Ivan was nodding at her as if she weren't his friend but only the thirteen-year-old baby-sitter. Next thing she knew, she'd be stuck with Doe while Miles and Ivan drank beer or went for a swim.

Miles shifted his weight from one foot to another. "Listen, Laur," he said. "Be home by six. Okay?"

Laurel dug her fingernails into the chicken. No, it was not okay. Not being checked on or being told for a second time, like a child, what time to be home.

"Nice of you to come over just for that," Ivan said. "I'm sure Laurel appreciates it. But — wait — before you go, tell me something."

"Sure," Miles said.

"Do you read the papers?"

"Sure. We get the Minneapolis paper by mail."

Ivan smiled engagingly. "You do? Terrific. I haven't seen one in weeks. So what's going on out there?"

"Nothing interesting except the Twins," Miles replied. "They've got a streak going."

"Oh, really? So they're hot, are they?"

Laurel swayed in the doorway of the cabin. Behind her she could hear snuffling noises. Doe was waking up, rattling the bars of her crib to attract attention. Laurel hadn't decided how they should cook the chicken, and now she had the baby to take care of, too.

"Is that Doe?" Ivan asked, turning away from Miles.

"Yes," she answered.

Ivan stared at Laurel for a moment. Then he winked. She was puzzled. She didn't know what was going on. "I'll get the baby," she said halfheartedly.

"No, no," Ivan insisted. "Let me. I'll do it, and I'll get your brother to tell me how the Twins are doing. Maybe I'll stick Doe on my back and walk him part of the way back to your place. So don't worry about the kitchen stuff. I can figure it out, you know. Why don't you go canoeing or something? Just keep track of the time and make sure you're home by six."

Suddenly Laurel understood everything. Because Ivan didn't want to irritate her brother, he was playing another game. A game called "Let's Impress Miles." And he was very good at it. She was barely able to nod before she turned and ran toward the kitchen. Once there, she stifled her laughter with a damp dish towel.

ELEVEN

Ivan creaked back and forth in the rocking chair as he read to his daughter. Doe patted the cardboard pages solemnly. "Be," she said, "be-be-be."

"Laurel?" Ivan called. "She's pointing to a picture of a baby. Do you think she's beginning to put sounds and words together? Yes, little girl, ba-by. Ba-by."

Laurel poked at the uncooked pork chops. She frowned. "Sometimes I think that Doe pays more attention to pictures than to voices."

"No, she doesn't," Ivan said. "I'm sure she doesn't, or if she does, it's her artistic temperament beginning to develop. Aren't babies amazing? Isn't Doe wonderful?"

As Ivan whistled and clucked and chuckled his way through the alphabet book, Laurel turned back to the food. A turkey had a big cavity in the middle to put the dressing in. Why couldn't she figure out how to get stuffing into the middle of the chops? Why did Doe keep saying "be-be" when most babies said "ma-ma" or "da-da" first?

The chicken had been the first of a series of dinners Laurel had fixed with Ivan, but the cooking wasn't getting any easier. It also didn't give her the satisfaction that learning to care for a baby did.

Usually, with Ivan's help, she prepared dinner just before she went home, so she wasn't around to see if he liked it. Tonight was different, however. Miles had driven to Minneapolis to meet Jessica. He was going to fly home for two weeks while Jessica came to stay with Laurel. She wouldn't arrive until noon tomorrow.

Laurel hadn't asked for permission to come and have dinner with Ivan. Instead, after Miles had left, she'd simply walked back to the cabin. Ivan hadn't questioned her presence. When she had told him she could stay late, he'd just said that it would be nice to have someone to talk to at dinner.

Earlier, Ivan — insisting that he liked a lot of stuffing — had prepared two packages of dressing mix. Now, looking at it, Laurel realized that there would be too much to wedge into a dozen chops. Frustrated, she finally decide to heap the dressing into a casserole and toss the chops on top of it. After shoving the whole thing into the oven, she rotated the dial on the gas stove to the 350 degrees recommended by the cookbook. Then she began to clean up the grit that had spilled on both the counter and the floor.

Sitting Doe on his shoulders, Ivan stood up and crunched over to the sink. "Would you mind," he asked, "if I put Ducky to bed and went out to work for a while?"

"No, that's fine," Laurel answered, watching as his boots tracked the crumbs into a wider area. "I'll keep an eye on her."

As soon as Ivan banged out of the cabin, Laurel reached for the broom. The oven was hissing. Her chops had a peculiar smell. She wondered if she had used too much sage.

As she tried to decide, she scooped crumbs onto a piece of newspaper. Somehow the broom slipped, and its handle knocked into a bottle of apple juice Ivan had left on the counter. When the bottle hit the floor, it shattered. Apple juice splattered in every direction. Doe started to cry.

For a moment, Laurel stood helplessly in the middle of the kitchen. She was barefooted. Glass was everywhere. The baby was screaming. She didn't know what to do first — take care of the broken glass, the baby, or dinner, which was smelling worse and worse.

But before she could make a decision, Ivan burst into the cabin. "Get out," he gasped. "Out immediately!" Without asking why, Laurel ran toward the back door. Almost instanteously, Ivan appeared carrying Doe. As soon as he had pushed her into Laurel's arms, he dove back into the cabin.

Laurel was frightened. Was something really wrong? Or was this another one of Ivan's games? But it wasn't a game. Ivan was opening all the windows. Then, coughing, he ran back outside.

Grabbing hold of the baby, he looked at her eyes and into her mouth. He thumped on her back. Finally, he spoke. "She's fine, just fine," he murmured, turning to Laurel. "Are you?"

"Of course . . . except — what's wrong?"

Ivan shook his head. "Lord, you're so competent, so helpful I forget. Gas, Laurel. G-a-s. With an ancient stove like ours, you always have to check the pilot light. It was out. You could have done us in. But — hey — wait. No tears, honey. It's all right. We're all fine."

Her stomach felt queasy. "You're sure everything's okay?" she asked.

"Sure, I'm sure. No sweat. In a minute or two the place will be aired out. Then we can

light the oven, put the kid to bed, and —
what's wrong with your feet?"

Laurel looked down. Her feet were bleed-
ing. She must have cut them on the broken
glass as she bolted out of the cabin. "They
don't hurt," she said.

"Well, we'll take care of them anyway."

When Ivan had investigated and determined that the cabin was safe, he put Doe in
her bed. Then he lifted Laurel, carried her
across the kitchen, and sat her on the counter.
As Laurel clenched her teeth together, he
probed and washed the cuts on the bottoms of
her feet with alcohol.

When the stinging subsided, she managed
to speak. "Doe," she said, "is lucky to have
you for a father."

"Sometimes I wonder," he replied, with a
shake of his head. "Okay, hold still. Good. Yes.
Look, there's nothing much wrong here. Wish
I knew as much about healing other things
as I do about cuts."

As he spoke, he used a tweezers to remove
a sliver from the ball of her right foot. His
fingers moved with the same skill he used on
the blocks of wood. "I'm always getting cuts
and splinters from tools and such. It's the invisible knives I can't stop or cure. Here —

look, only this gash under your big toe is deep enough to bandage."

Laurel listened quietly. She was happy to have him bent over, working, talking. She knew her feet were all right, but she liked being taken care of.

"There," Ivan said, indicating he had finished doctoring her. He smiled at Laurel in a way that made her shiver.

She looked down. "I should do something about the mess on the floor," she said, attempting to disguise the awkwardness she felt.

"No, you don't," Ivan insisted. "You stay right where you are. I'll light the oven, put dinner in, and then I'll do the floor. That's an order. Okay?"

"Okay," she agreed.

So, as Laurel watched, Ivan took care of everything. A savory smell began to fill the kitchen. The pork chops were cooking and soon she and Ivan would sit down to dinner together. He swept carefully, but he didn't mop as she would have done. As long as he was sure there weren't any glass chips to cut his daughter, sticky floors didn't bother him.

"Where are we going to eat?" she asked, speaking softly so she wouldn't awaken Doe.

Ivan put the broom away. Then he cleared

off the table. "How's that? Okay? But we don't have to whisper, really. Once Doe falls asleep at night, that's it. She's out. I can play music or whatever I want and nothing disturbs her."

Laurel slid off the counter. As she took forks and knives from the dishrack, she wrinkled her nose. "It smells like something's burning." When she opened the oven door, the smell was worse.

"The chops look shriveled," Ivan said, as he came up behind her. In addition, the dressing had swelled and spilled onto the bottom of the oven. Laurel groaned. As soon as one mess was cleared away, they had another on their hands.

"What happened?" she asked. "I may have put in too much, but that shouldn't make it burn."

Ivan gulped. Then he laughed. *"Mea culpa. I'm guilty.* I turned the dial up because I thought dinner would cook faster."

Laurel checked the dial. It was turned past 500. Ivan was even worse in the kitchen than she was. Laughing, trying not to think how hard it would be when they had to scrub the oven, she took two potholders and lifted the smoking casserole from the oven. "If you finish with the table, I'll dish this out."

"Okay," Ivan agreed, rummaging through

the drawer that held supplies for emergency power outages. When he'd found a pair of candles, he went outside and picked wild-flowers to decorate the table.

Soon the two of them, their plates filled with half-burned dressing and dried-out chops, sat across from one another in the candlelit cabin. Their dinner tasted as un-appetizing as it looked, but Laurel had stopped worrying about food because she had a new problem. She and Ivan didn't seem to have anything to talk about. When she saw Ivan staring moodily at his plate, she shifted uncomfortably in her chair. Why was it she seemed to have so little to say? What, Laurel asked herself, *did* people talk about all the time? What would it be like to be married?

When she moved again, her chair scraped against the bare wooden floor. Ivan looked up. He frowned. "Is something wrong?" he asked.

Using a fork, Laurel raked through the stuffing on her plate. "Mmm . . . not really. It's just — well, I was trying to figure out what married people talk about at dinner."

Ivan nodded. "I used to wonder that my-self, and then Allison used to prattle inces-santly sometimes, until I just wanted to tell her to shut up. Sometimes I even did. Allison thought conversation made dinner better."

"If her cooking was as bad as ours, it probably didn't," Laurel commented.

Ivan chuckled. "You're good company, Laurel, and you're not afraid of silence. I like silence. I suppose that's why it's hard for me to keep remembering that I need to talk to Doe. You know, sometimes I think we all talk too much. Maybe Adam and Eve were expelled from Eden not for tasting the apple but for talking too much."

"Mmm . . ." Laurel agreed.

"Every once in a while I'll have a dream about a carving or something — and it'll be so intense it sticks with me for days, preoccupying me so that I can hardly bear to hear people talk. Do you know what I mean? Do you have dreams like that?"

"Mmm . . . sometimes," Laurel said.

"I'm sure it has something to do with spatial awareness. My mother would know."

Laurel leaned forward. Ivan had never mentioned any member of his family before. "Your mother?"

"My mother . . ." Ivan mused. He put a large bite of chop into his mouth. He chewed on it methodically. Then he swallowed. "But I can't ask her, you see, because she's dead. She died of cancer five years ago. My brother, Bud, is the only family I have left. But he lives in Seattle, and I haven't seen him since her funeral."

"And your father?"

"He left us when I was mine. He's down South somewhere. Irony of ironies, I always swore it wouldn't happen to me. I was going to be part of a real family. Have it all — family and adventure. Now look at me — making a mess out of everything. God, I wanted that real family so badly. Then Allison — "

Ivan's unfinished sentence floated over the table between them. "Then Allison *what*?" Laurel wanted to ask. "What *did* Allison do? Why aren't you together?" But she trapped her tongue between her teeth.

"See, that's just what I mean," Ivan told her.

Laurel frowned. "Huh?"

"About silence. You offer company without pressure. It's wonderful to have you around, Laurel. I don't feel nearly so alone. Just what would I have done without you these last weeks? Shh, don't answer that. I always know I can count on you."

TWELVE

Outside, the sun hovered low on the horizon. As Ivan and Laurel ate, they watched it through the window. Ivan continued to do most of the talking, but Laurel didn't mind. She listened.

Once they had eaten what they could, they scraped the rest of the food into the garbage can. Then, together, they washed the dishes and scrubbed out the charred oven. As they worked, Laurel hummed quietly to herself. She wanted to tell Ivan how happy she felt, how important he — and Doe — were to her. But she was afraid that if she started talking, she'd sound like Allison. Silence was better. Ivan was right. If she didn't say anything, she wouldn't make any embarrassing mistakes.

When the kitchen was clean, Ivan fixed cups of tea. Then they went outside to watch the sunset. Laurel didn't usually drink tea but taking it made her feel more adult. Holding the mug with both hands, she sat on the stump.

After Ivan prowled around examining his carvings for a while, he turned to her. "I'd like to do one of you, Laurel," he said. "Maybe more than one. I'd start with small clay pieces. I'd like to try to catch you fawn-like and capture that wistful, self-contained quality you have."

Laurel felt herself flush. She took a swallow of tea. She was glad that it was too dark for him to get a better look at her. This was the first time he'd suggested she was a good subject for his work.

"Maybe even one of you and Doe."

"I'd like that," Laurel said, trying to keep her voice from sounding too childishly enthusiastic.

"Good. Terrific. But I'll need to do some planning before I can start," Ivan told her, as he seated himself near the stump. When he leaned back, his left shoulder was close to Laurel's right leg. Not knowing why, she moved her leg closer. Then, reconsidering, she shifted away again. She scanned the woods around them, wondering if Spencer was lurking nearby listening. No, she decided, he'd be at work at the gas station.

"Forget Spencer," she told herself.

She looked at the sun, poised across the lake for its descent behind the pine forest. Its rays stabbed the purpled clouds ranged on the horizon. As Laurel lowered her eyes, something odd occurred to her. She wanted to touch the top of Ivan's head.

Before she had time to act on her impulse, however, Ivan sprang to his feet. "Let's do something," he suggested. "Quickly, before the sun goes down. For some reason I'm bursting with energy. Let's take out the canoe."

Laurel put down her mug. "How can we? Didn't you say we weren't going to leave Doe alone anymore?"

"Yes, I did. But come on — let's. Just one last time. Then no more — I promise. Okay? We'll check on her before we go. We'll stay right in the cove here, and if she even peeps we'll hear her."

The sun had dipped below the horizon, but the sky was still suffused with light. Golds and pinks and purples spread in the sky and puddled on the water around them. It was beautiful, breathtakingly beautiful, Laurel thought. Better than cities or schools. Better than books or proms or jobs.

Ivan dipped his paddle quietly. At his insistence, Laurel wasn't paddling. She sat in the bow, watching the world around her color, then slowly darken. She'd seen the same sun set over the same lake hundreds of times in her life. She'd never listened when her family urged her to appreciate it. Perhaps part of the secret was having someone other than family to watch it with. She wanted to ask Ivan about this, but she didn't.

Maybe, sitting behind her in the stern of the canoe, he was wishing he had someone else floating with him on Hoop Lake. Laurel glanced back. Ivan didn't look unhappy. He looked contented. When he saw her examining him, he sent her a quick smile. "Your hair's nice," he said.

Running one hand over the top of her French braid, she returned the smile. Then she lowered her eyes. She didn't want him to see how much she liked his compliment.

"Maybe, when St. Exupéry wrote *Wind, Sand, and Stars*, he had a canoe in mind when he spoke about looking outward in the same direction," Ivan said.

A mosquito whined somewhere near Laurel's head. She swatted at it.

"Or swimming, night swimming," Ivan continued. "Let's check on Doe, get towels. Let's. . . ."

Laurel was too delighted to protest; and

soon she and Ivan were floating in the cove
below the cabin. She felt light, weightless.
She wanted this night to go on forever.
Treading water, she watched as the stars
began to appear in the sky above them. Ivan
swam out toward the sandbar. After a while
he came in closer again. He dived under the
water. Laurel expected him to grab her feet
from below, but he didn't.

"What an evening," he sputtered as he
surfaced a short distance away. "Almost perfect."

"Mmm . . ." she agreed.

"I'd like the moon, though. Or northern
lights."

Laurel giggled. "The best place to see them
up here is the drive-in. They streak like
flames from behind the screen."

"I'd rather watch them across the lake.
More aesthetic. But it's too early, I think.
They come closer to midnight, don't they?
It's not that late. Not nearly."

As Ivan spoke, Laurel rolled over and lay
on her back. Water stopped up her ears, but
she didn't change position. She was waiting
for something. Waiting, perhaps, for him to
pick her up and toss her the way Miles would
have. Instead, he swam in widening circles
around her. Laurel wrapped her arms about

her knees. She sank below the surface of the water. Slowly, she began to let tiny bubbles of air escape. Then there was no more air, just pressure on her chest, more and more pressure. It was quiet down there. Even quieter than above. Almost unbearably quiet. She shot up to the surface.

"Where were you?" Ivan asked. "One minute you were there, then the next you were gone. Don't scare me like that. I don't want to lose you. You're much too precious."

He'd been worried about her. Pleased, Laurel sprayed a mouthful of water in the direction of his voice. Though his head was bobbing nearby, she couldn't see the expression on his face. She waited for him to spit back, but he didn't.

"Ivan?" she asked tentatively. She wanted to try to describe how she was feeling.

"I'm here," he answered. He was close, yet he sounded as if he were far away. "I'm here. . . ."

"Ivan. . . ."

"What, dear?"

"I want to say something. I want — "

As Laurel groped for the right words, suddenly Ivan turned and began to wade from the water. "Don't go. Please stay," she wanted to say, but her voice stuck in her throat. She lowered her feet, let them brush the sandy bottom of the lake. Disappointed, she waded out after him.

He threw her a towel. Shivering, she wrapped herself in it. Ivan stood a few feet away. As far as he was concerned, their swim was over. Though she was sure that he wanted her to pull her clothes on and go home, she wasn't ready to leave. The moment for speaking was gone. It had burst in her face like a soap bubble, but — still — she was waiting for something.

"Get a move on," Ivan urged, "before the mosquitoes eat us alive. No matter how peaceful you think you feel, there's always something trying to nibble at you. Nibble, nibble. . . ."

Yes, the mosquitoes were swarming about them. She'd hardly noticed. Responding to Ivan's words, she put her cutoffs and shirt on over her suit. Her bandaged toe ached as she wedged it into her sneakers. She was shivering and her braid lay limply against her neck. Maybe, she thought, Ivan would throw an arm around her shoulder and invite her in for a cup of hot chocolate.

Slapping at mosquitoes, jumping up and down, Laurel hesitated. A cry broke the silence.

"Loons?" Ivan asked.

"Loons," she replied. "They sound like crazy people or like crying babies."

Ivan's towel hung cape-like from his shoulders. "I'd walk you home," he said, "but I don't think I should leave the baby. It's been nice — nice to have her sleeping, to have time to breathe, to feel like a real person again, instead of only like a guardian keeping her safe from danger."

Laurel backed up. She looked at Ivan standing beside her. She didn't want this evening to end. She was beginning to realize why she'd been waiting. She wanted Ivan to do something. She hoped he would indicate how he felt about her, say that he wanted her close to him. Not just for tonight, but on and on. If she could stay with Ivan, she could skip high school, skip those years and the difficult decisions that came after. She and Ivan could stay peacefully at Hoop Lake, having adventures, raising Doe together.

It was a startling and wonderful thought. She didn't simply like Ivan. She loved him. He wasn't a boyfriend but someone she could love and live with. She didn't want to say this aloud. It was too risky. Maybe it was too soon. Maybe, if she waited a few more weeks, he'd tell her he loved her and wanted her to stay. Well, she could wait. That was worth waiting for.

But something else wasn't. Now, with a flash of insight, she knew what else she'd been expecting — Ivan's touch. Usually he touched her as he touched Doe, but not tonight. Trying to read the expression on his face, she squinted. Did he feel some of, any of, what she felt?

"You won't lose your way in the dark?" he asked.

"I won't lose my way," Laurel replied.

Still, she lingered. At last, impulsively, she stepped forward and put her arms around Ivan's neck. For a moment, he didn't respond. Then he patted her on the back. When he hugged her, it was in a gentle, restrained way, over almost before it had begun.

"So that's the way it is, little caterpillar," he murmured. "I should have guessed. I should have known. Don't hurry it. Don't worry, you will turn into a butterfly. In due time."

When he had finished speaking, he leaned forward. Hands at his sides, he kissed her on the ear. His beard, surprisingly soft, brushed her cheek. Then he gave Laurel's shoulder a push. She needed no more encouragement. Shaking, she started to run. Twigs crackled under her feet. Her heart pounded. Something wonderful was beginning. Something mysterious. She was in love with Ivan.

But, for now, she had to listen to him, go as slowly as he wanted. Maybe *he* was waiting for something. For August, for her fourteenth birthday. In any case, Ivan knew what was happening. Because it was happening to him, too.

Faster, Laurel ran. Then faster. The sky seemed brighter than it had before. She wondered if, after all, the northern lights were shining.

THIRTEEN

Doe sat in her playpen poring over her cardboard books. "Ba-ba-ba," she said. "Be-be-be-be-be." Laurel waved at her. Then she turned back and began to reexamine the directions on the can of floor wax.

Laurel had neither a sponge mop nor a buffer. If she intended to wax the floor, she had to improvise. Last night she and Ivan had shared dinner, a canoe ride, and a swim. It had been a night Laurel would never forget because she and Ivan were falling in love. Now, the next morning, she had returned to the cabin with two resolves — the floor would be shined, and she would make Doe love her as much as Ivan did.

Her life was about to change, yet she wasn't sure how to tell her family. She knew they wouldn't approve. They'd criticize — say she was too young, that she was being unrealistic, that she had to stay in school. But she wouldn't listen to them. Most of the time, her mother and the others were too busy with their own lives to understand hers. Well, let them keep on being busy. Then they wouldn't miss her when she stayed on with Ivan and Doe. And if the three of them were going to share this cabin, something had to be done about the floor. As Laurel mulled this over, she checked to see what Doe was doing.

Satisfied that the child was still absorbed in her books, Laurel turned back to the can of wax. She'd decided to work on the floor first because it seemed to be the simpler of her two resolutions. What she really wanted to do, however, was stay outside close to Ivan.

But he had been distant when she'd appeared. She'd shrugged it off because he was often that way when he was at work. Besides, this morning he had a new log propped against the stump. Chips of wood flew through the air as he attacked it with rapid yet delicate taps. When she trotted up behind him, he barely acknowledged her presence. Although disappointed, Laurel accepted this. If she was going to live with him, she must — even if it was hard — respect his work and his ideas about silence. It seemed a small sacrifice for what she would be gaining.

As Laurel dribbled the first drops of wax

onto the cracked linoleum, Doe stood up and began to shake the bars of the playpen. "Hold on, little girl," Laurel said, using her most soothing tone. "Not yet. Come on. You can play there longer. I know you can." Using the broom, she began to spread the wax over the floor. "So be good, please."

Doe did not respond to Laurel's coaxing. Protesting, she sent up rattling noises from deep in her throat. Then she began to empty the playpen of its contents. "Go ahead. Have fun," Laurel told her as she poured out more wax and renewed her efforts with the broom. By the time everything was thrown overboard, the floor would be done.

Laurel was able to ignore the tumbling toys until Doe skidded her terry-cloth teddy bear into a pool of wax, then, gritting her teeth, she retrieved the animal. With babies and kitchens, she was learning, nothing ever got done without unexpected problems cropping up. Well, she'd get used to it. She moved the playpen farther away from the doorway of the kitchen. "There," she said. "Fooled you, girl. What do you have to say now?"

The words were hardly out of her mouth when Doe answered, expressing her displeasure with a series of high-pitched wails. In a minute, Ivan would appear to ask what was going on. Laurel looked around. The floor was only half done; Ivan's breakfast dishes were stacked in the sink. Discouraged, she dropped the broom and hurried over to pick up the baby.

Doe's diapers were soaked, but she didn't want them changed. As Laurel battled with her, Doe tugged at her hair. "So pull it, then," Laurel told her. "Anything, just so I can get you cleaned up."

Ivan had diapered the baby carelessly, so Laurel had to wash her and change her shirt and overalls, too. By the time the baby was dressed again, hunks of Laurel's hair hung limply about her face. Because she wanted to redo her braid before she saw Ivan, she lowered Doe back into the playpen. But the moment her feet touched its wooden bottom, Doe started to cry again.

This time Ivan reacted immediately. "Hey, is everyone all right?" he called.

"Yes, yes . . ." Laurel assured him, lunging for the baby.

"You sure? I'll come if you want. But I'm at a crucial spot — one slip and the whole block of wood is ruined. Do you need me?"

"No," she said. "No . . . everything's fine."

She bounced Doe up and down in her arms. She was sorry that Ivan had been disturbed.

"Be-be-be," Doe commanded, struggling to free herself. "Be-be-be-be!"

"No," Laurel told her impatiently. "But I'll read to you. How about that? Books, huh? Maybe I can teach you to say something. Dad-dy, say daddy. Come on, Doe. What's wrong, little girl, huh? Why are you such a fussbudget?"

Doe didn't want to be distracted. She wanted to find her father. Despite the coolness of the morning, Laurel was overheated. "I'm not very good at this stuff," she murmured. "Maybe, Doe-baby, I'd better take you for a walk."

Laurel didn't ask Ivan's permission or Doe's, either. Feeling harassed, she was struggling to get both the baby and the carrier onto her back when a familiar voice broke into her consciousness.

"Hello, there. Hello. I'm looking for my sister."

Laurel gulped. It was Jessica. She'd arrived already, and Ivan's work was going to be disturbed. With the baby under one arm and the carrier under the other, Laurel stepped out of the door.

"Well, what have we here?" Jessica asked.

Laurel managed to send her sister a wan smile. Jessica was wearing white tennis shorts and a white shirt. Her dark hair, every lock in place, swayed gently as she strode uphill from the beach.

"I came by canoe," she said. "God, it feels great to be back at the lake. Don't you just love it here?"

Her question was addressed to Ivan. As she spoke, she extended one hand and moved forward. "I'm Jessica Tavrow," she said.

Ivan put his tools down on the stump and reached out for her hand. "Ivan," he offered, smiling in the friendly, offhand manner that Laurel liked so much.

Jessica made a face. "Ivan? Just Ivan? Don't you have a last name, Ivan?"

Ivan shrugged. He dropped Jessica's hand. "Well, yes . . . sure. I'm Ivan Wood."

"Wood? That's funny," Jessica said. "Quite wonderful, really — Ivan Wood sculpts in wood. A fine irony, don't you think?"

Leaning his head to one side, Ivan nodded. "A fine irony," he agreed.

Laurel was relieved that Ivan didn't seem to be upset because of the interruption. "Ivan Wood," she told herself. "Ivan Wood." She loved him, was planning to move in with him, and she had never asked his last name. "Well, it's not really important," she told herself, dropping the carrier and hitching the baby higher on her hip. Then she brushed some of her unkempt hair out of her face.

Doe squirmed. "Be-be-be," she insisted.

Turning, Ivan reached out for the baby. "Here, I'll take her."

Ivan's hands brushed against hers as he took hold of Doe. Laurel was at his side facing Jessica. She was glad to see her sister, happy that she seemed to like Ivan. As Laurel stood there, she hoped Ivan would rest a hand on her shoulder. He winked at Laurel, but he kept both hands wrapped around his daughter.

After a moment, Jessica reached out and tickled Doe under the chin. A wary half smile flickered across the child's face.

Ivan grinned. "Well, look at that, Jessica Tavrow. My daughter doesn't waste her smiles on just anybody. Consider yourself privileged."

Clenching her fists, Laurel tried not to feel jealous.

"Could I hold the baby?" Jessica asked. "Would she come to me? Have you ever tried putting a bow in her hair?"

"What hair?" Ivan asked, laughing.

"Now, don't talk that way. Tell your daddy not to malign you that way, young woman. She has hair — reddish, too. I think she's going to be a real beauty."

Laurel made a face. Jessica wasn't interested in babies. She'd never cared about them — any more than Laurel had.

As Laurel watched, Jessica took hold of Doe. Turning in a circle, she bounced the baby up and down. Then, suddenly, she stopped before Laurel. "You look like you've been through a tornado."

"She has," Ivan said. "Doe is a tornado."

"Doe?" Jessica said, wrinkling her nose. "That's not a *name*. What's your *real* name, Baby Doe?"

"Saskia," Laurel offered.

"Saskia? Like Rembrandt's mistress, Saskia?" her sister asked. "An unusual name and yet — I read about a Saskia. Last week somewhere."

Ivan tapped his mallet against the stump.

"Yes," Jessica continued, "I know I read something, but — yes, what is it, little Saskia? Oh-ho, so you want to walk, huh? You want to get down and walk to Daddy."

Jessica put the baby on her feet.

"Don't do that," Laurel said. "Ivan doesn't like to have her held that way."

"Oh, it's all right," Ivan said. "I suppose she's old enough now."

"I don't remember where I saw the name . . ." Jessica mused, holding Doe's hands and letting her step toward her father.

"Does it matter?" Ivan asked. "Life, I've noticed, is made up of coincidences. As if it were preordained that you would read about a Saskia, then meet one. Well, in any case, welcome. You can, if you wish — now that I've prepared this log — watch me make my first cuts."

Jessica let go of Doe's fingers. The baby plopped down onto her bottom. "First cuts?"

"Into a new block," Ivan said, taking up a plane and using it to produce pale, sweet-smelling curls of wood. "I have this vision that the whole finished sculpture preexists inside. It's Michelangelo's concept — credited to him, yet no one has a source to prove he really said it. And so — my job then is to un-peel the form carefully, without spoiling it."

"It's like that in designs, too," Jessica said, with a toss of her head. "I'm still in school, but when I draft plans, I always feel that way about a building. Cautious — and for the exact same reason."

Jessica didn't seem perplexed by anything Ivan said. For what seemed like a long time, Laurel listened to conversation flow back and forth between them.

Suddenly, though, something caught Laurel's eye. "The baby. Get her quick. She's putting wood chips into her mouth."

When neither Jessica nor Ivan reacted quickly enough, Laurel sprang forward. She pried Doe's mouth open and probed with her finger. "No," she scolded. "Not in your mouth.

Bad girl. Do you hear me? That's dir-ty. *Dirty*. Not for Doe."

Jessica bent down to take a look. "Hey, Pokey, you're good at that."

Ivan grinned. "She sure is. The best."

Laurel flushed as she waited for Ivan to offer more praise. Instead of complimenting her, though, he spoke to her sister. "It just takes practice. A lot of practice."

Jessica lifted Doe to her feet again. "Then maybe I'll try my hand at it, too. Come here, little darling."

While Laurel watched, Jessica managed to play with Doe and talk to Ivan at the same time. Soon Ivan began to demonstrate how he worked. As he angled a gouge and tapped on it, he told Jessica what he was doing. At first Laurel was fascinated. These were things she'd never learned from Ivan. Then she realized that his tone was different from the one she was used to.

Soon Laurel knew that she didn't want to listen anymore. She felt left out. She tried to remember how Ivan had been last night, in the dark, at the beach. It seemed hazy and far away. Then she attempted to figure out what was happening now. Was Ivan, to impress Jessica, playing another one of his games? He didn't seem to be faking, however. He seemed sincere.

Wordlessly, Laurel turned and went back into the kitchen. Unspread wax stuck to the bottoms of her feet. It had congealed into globs, making the floor look worse than before. She couldn't smooth it out or wipe it up. When she tried to wash the bear, it lay on the drainboard, staring at her with bright eyes and a stiff face.

FOURTEEN

The sounds of Jessica's light voice and Ivan's low one drifted through the open window. Laurel stood on her tiptoes so she could look out. In almost the same breath, Ivan spoke of Allison and of sculpting. Gesturing expansively, he even reached over and touched Jessica's arm.

Jessica was kneeling on the stump looking like some kind of beautiful sculpture. Laurel's stomach tightened. She didn't like what she was seeing or what she heard. Ivan had accepted Jessica's company as readily as he accepted hers. Laurel's eyes stung. She wanted to cry as Doe cried, howl as Doe howled. But then, all of a sudden, she realized something. The scene framed in the window had everything except the baby.

"Where's Doe?" she called.

"What?" Ivan asked.

"Where's Doe?" she repeated, running outside.

"Doe? I thought she was — oh, no . . . the water. . . ."

But Doe had not headed for the water. She had crawled off into the woods, where they found her sitting placidly by a clump of poison ivy.

"Poison ivy," Ivan exclaimed as he lifted her up. "How could we have been so stupid? Get one of the books, Laurel, and look it up."

"We don't need books," Laurel told him. "We just need to wash her with yellow soap."

"Soap?" Ivan asked incredulously. "What's soap going to do?"

"Laurel's right," Jessica said. "Lava soap has always been our cure-all for exposure to poison ivy."

Ivan shook his head. "But I don't have any. And it's going to take time to drive and — "

"Never mind," Laurel told him as she reached out for the baby. She was angry at them and at herself for being careless with Doe. "I'll look after her. I'll get soap at the Harrisons', and she'll be fine."

Before Ivan could object, Laurel marched off with the baby. As she hurried along the path, she berated herself. If she was thinking of staying with Ivan, of taking care of Doe like a mother, then she could not be guilty of lapses like that. A good mother, unlike Laurel's own, *always* had to pay attention. As she imagined Allison had done. . . .

When Laurel reached the Harrison house, Spencer was outside sawing on a two-by-four. "Where's the yellow soap?" she asked him. "The baby got into poison ivy."

Spencer put down the saw. He went into the garage and returned with a bar of yellowish-brown soap. Then, acting helpful yet not alarmed, he spoke. "Let's use the kitchen sink. Come on, baldy. It's bathtime."

While Laurel stripped the baby, Spencer filled the sink with warm water. He tested the temperature with his elbow. "It's fine. Pop her in."

"How did you know to do *that*?" Laurel asked.

"Cousins," he replied. "I have dozens of them. And Mom, she checks everything with her elbow around kids — ovens, bathwater — the works. You'll learn. You might have learned earlier, of course, when we played Druids, except we never had any Druid babies, did we?"

Instead of answering, Laurel lowered Doe into the sink and began to lather her up. Doe stared at Laurel and Spencer as they scrubbed her skin until it turned pink. She didn't cry, but she didn't smile, either.

"Funny kid," Spencer remarked. "Do you think there's something wrong with her? Is she a little retarded or something?"

"No!" Laurel exclaimed. "What do you know? How can you say that?"

Spencer produced a kitchen towel and two safety pins to diaper Doe. "Well, she is quiet." He shrugged. "She's not real friendly, either. Not even to you, and you've been looking after her for weeks."

Laurel wanted to argue with him, but she knew he was right. There was something unusual about Doe, even if she'd never figured out what it was.

When Spencer saw Laurel struggling with the pins, he pushed her aside and took over. "Yes, I know — the throwaway ones you use have glue or something on them. Well, Uncle Spencer knows about diapers, and he also knows what little kiddies like, doesn't he? Like music, for instance."

The next thing Laurel knew, Spencer had whisked Doe off to the Harrisons' upright piano. He showed her how to pound on the keys. At first, the baby slapped tentatively at the treble keys. Not willing to give up, Spencer shifted her in front of the bass keys. Suddenly her eyes opened wide and she began to blink and pound.

"I did it," Spencer said proudly. "See."

Laurel sat down next to him. He had helped out. He was good with Doe, but she couldn't really tell him that because Doe was pounding on the keyboard.

After a while, uncomfortable at being seated next to Spencer, Laurel rose to her feet. She lifted Doe's hands away from the piano. "I think," she said, "we'd better go. Ivan and Jessica are back at the cabin. They'll be worrying."

Doe screwed up her face as if she was going to cry.

"Worrying?" Spencer asked, making faces to distract the baby. "Oh, I bet they'll be worrying. Ivan doesn't strike me as a worrier. There's something weird about him. How could his wife have let him come up here with a baby? Doesn't *she* worry?"

"Cut it out," Laurel said. Was Spencer right? Did Allison worry? Should she be worried? "What do you know?"

"I know what I see. And now wonderful Jessica, the love of my life, has appeared. Better and better. Or worse and worse. Maybe we should all go to the drive-in. Because now it's going to be Laurel and Ivan *and* Jessica. The plot is thickening! But you can't see it because you have a crush on that guy."

"Shut up!" Laurel said. "Shut up!"

A crush? She didn't have a crush on Ivan.

She knew the difference between having a crush and being in love. But Spencer was too immature. Trouble — that's what she got for letting her guard down, for acting as if he were a normal human being. There was no use trying to explain anything to him. So, without thanking Spencer or saying goodbye, she left.

If Laurel had expected Ivan and Jessica to be impatient for her return, she had been mistaken. When she — with Doe lolling in her arms — approached the cabin, she found them sprawled in the sun drinking lemonade.

Curious, Laurel lingered at the edge of the clearing listening as they discussed commitments to relationships in and out of marriage. She wanted to be part of their conversation, but she didn't know how. Besides, it was time for Doe's lunch and the kitchen floor needed work. Laurel examined Ivan. He was strong and handsome-looking with that curly red beard of his. He was full of ideas for new adventures. How could Spencer find him strange or suspicious?

Laurel knew she was eavesdropping, but she stood there anyway. How, she wondered, would Allison feel if she were standing watching them? Suspicious? Unhappy? Laurel wished she could close her eyes and make Jessica disappear. Jessica was an intruder. Laurel wanted to be lying on the grass with Ivan and Doe. It would be fine with her if no one else entered their private world. But it probably wouldn't suit Ivan. He liked people; and besides, why shouldn't he have fun with Jessica?

"Because," she whispered, answering her own question with an unaccustomed burst of fierceness, "he's mine. That's why."

FIFTEEN

Raindrops chased one another down the windowpane as Laurel waited for Jessica to move. Jessica had already captured her queen, so she couldn't imagine what was taking so long. Laurel wanted to jump to her feet and deliberately turn over the chessboard, as she had done when she was a child.

But biting down on her lip, she sat there in silence. Jessica had told her it was too wet to go to Ivan's, that she had to stay home until the Sunday storm blew over. Since her sister had arrived a week ago, she'd had little time alone with Ivan. Her only consolation was savoring the notion that soon the two of them would be together. Then her family would not be able to boss her around.

She tried to picture Ivan lounging with her in the trapper's cabin as rain pelted against the roof. Closing her eyes, she attempted to imagine, instead, that it was December, with large flakes of snow settling on the pines as she and Ivan and Doe snuggled before a crackling fire. Some days she could reel these pictures through her head like a series of movie scenes. But this morning it was difficult. The dream she'd had last night was haunting her, interfering.

"I'm castling," Jessica said. Then, remembering something, she looked up. "Last night . . . what was it you were asking me about when I was falling asleep over my book. About love, wasn't it?"

Laurel sacrificed another pawn. She didn't know what had made her brave enough to bring up the subject. When her sister hadn't answered, she'd felt relieved.

"About how you know if it's true love?"

"Mmm . . . I guess," Laurel responded as casually as she could. What she wanted this morning was someone to talk with, not about love, but about her dream.

"Well, I don't know if I'm qualified. I've just come out of being involved with a real scumbag. And I don't think that was love . . . no. But I've been there, and what it's like is a tidal wave. You feel wonderful but totally powerless. You feel bubbling, as if you want to spend every minute with that person or thinking about him. He's a friend, of course, but more — so much more, because something inside keeps boiling up, saying, 'Hey, baby, *this is it.*' "

Jessica paused for a moment. She lined up the men she'd captured from her sister. Then she spoke again. "What made you ask?"

Before Laurel could decide how to respond, the front door flew open and a gust of wind chilled the room. Then the door slammed. When Laurel looked up, she saw Ivan standing on the rag rug. His head and red beard were dripping water. He was smiling. In his arms, draped in a plastic drop cloth, was Doe.

"Hello. Hello, everyone. Don't get up. I hope you don't mind me walking in like this. Funny, I even knew the door would be unlocked. And it was."

Laurel jumped to her feet. "What can I do? Should I take Doe? Didn't you get soaked?"

Ivan winked at her. "No, no, we're fine," he said. "We came by truck. Besides, I've always wanted to see this place. And look at it. You have a two-story fieldstone fireplace. Compared to our little cave, it's luxurious."

"Make yourself at home," Jessica said, kicking off her shoes. She yawned and stretched, smoothing out her rose-colored velour jumpsuit. Then she tucked her arms around her knees. If Laurel had suspected Ivan might show up, she would have worn something other than P.E. sweats, but now it was too late.

Ivan put Doe down on the couch. The baby's eyes were only half open. "She's sluggish today," Ivan commented. "She may have a fever. But she'll be better off here, I think. The cabin — even with a fire — is a drafty place when it storms."

"A fever?" Laurel asked. "Should we do something?"

Ivan propped the baby against his chest and straightened up. "I already did. She's had aspirin, so sleep is probably what she needs."

"Do you want me to hold her?" Laurel offered. "I'll rock her to sleep."

Laurel was aware that Jessica, saying nothing, was watching them. Had Ivan, appearing right after Jessica's description of being in love, made her suspicious? Laurel hoped not. She and Ivan needed more time together before anyone found out how they felt about each other.

Ivan's voice cut into her thoughts. "No. A bed will be fine. We don't want to spoil her. Besides, I have this strap thing that stretches around the mattress. Come on — find us a bed and I'll show you."

Laurel smiled. She didn't care what Jessica thought, especially when Ivan was speaking to her almost as if her sister weren't there. "This way. Doe can sleep in my room," she said as she headed down the corridor.

Her bed was unmade. Dirty clothes and underwear were piled in one corner. She was neat at the trapper's cabin, but that was for Ivan and Doe. At home, she was much less particular. She felt embarrassed, wishing she'd taken him to some other room. Ivan, however, didn't seem to notice.

He showed her how the white strap fitted tightly around the mattress. Then he stretched another set of straps around Doe, pinning them in the middle of her back with a large safety pin. "It works like this," he explained. "She's in the center and attached, but there's enough play for her to roll over in either direction. Clever, isn't it?" Ivan paused and stroked his beard. "One of Allison's ideas...."

Allison. Laurel didn't want to hear her name or think about her, yet no matter what she did, even if Ivan didn't mention her, Allison was close by. She floated in and out of Laurel's thoughts. Now she was part of Laurel's dreams, too....

On the end of a translucent string, a kite danced. It was a kite of intense color and iridescent beauty. But strange, too. If the wind that supported it made noise, Laurel couldn't hear it. The kite dipped and rose in silence.

"There, there," a woman's voice crooned. "Take care, take care. . . ."

The quiet kite, its tail flicking from side to side, mesmerized Laurel. Its gloriousness took her breath away. When, at last, she managed to wrench her eyes from the spectacle of the kite, she realized that the voice belonged to the woman who was flying it. The woman guided the string as if the kite were part of her, singing as she reeled the line or let it spin through her fingers. It was Allison — Laurel knew her because she looked just like the woman in Ivan's sculpture.

"Yes, yes," Allison breathed. "Fly, my love. Fly." Her voice spilled out, running on in the cadence of a song. She seemed to be singing a lullaby. Though Laurel strained, she couldn't understand the words.

Then suddenly the dream changed. Laurel was at a flea market, and Allison was standing next to her, handing her something. It was the kite — the same one that had soared overhead, but it was different now that it had been pulled out of the sky. The colors were muted. It had flaws, frayed spots that Laurel had not seen when it was above her head. And yet it was still beautiful. Laurel took it into her arms gently, lovingly, because she knew the strange, silent kite was something of value.

Laurel leaned toward Allison. "What do I owe you?" she whispered, holding the kite to her chest. "What do you want?"

Allison shook her head. She smiled wistfully, but she didn't answer.

And that was the dream. Even with her eyes open, Laurel saw Allison flying the kite, heard her crooning to it.

"Sleep, sleep. You're all right, little Saskia. . . ."

Laurel shuddered and turned her head. She was confusing last night's dream with what was really happening. It wasn't Allison she heard now but Ivan.

As he spoke to the baby, he knelt down next to the bed. "I think you're fine, honey . . . so sleep now, will you?"

Was Doe all right? Laurel wasn't sure. She frowned. There was something disturbing about the dream, about Doe that Laurel couldn't grasp. And Allison — Allison wanted something. What was it?

Laurel dropped down beside Ivan. She watched as he stroked Doe's head. "Sleepy-time, honey. Yes, and the rain should help. 'Rain, rain, go away. Come again another day. Little Doe wants to play. . . .' "

As his voice trailed off, Laurel leaned closer to him. " 'The rain is raining all around,' " she murmured, watching as Doe's eyes fluttered glassily. " 'It falls on field and tree. It falls on umbrellas here, and. . . .' "

" '. . . on the ships at sea,' " Ivan whispered, finishing the rhyme for her.

They both laughed. Doe's eyes snapped open for an instant. Then she closed them again.

"Hey, what's going on back there?" Jessica called from the living room.

Laurel started guiltily. For a moment she'd forgotten about her sister. Although she was not happy to be reminded, Ivan didn't seem to care. Putting a finger to his lips, he stood up.

As Ivan reached out and pulled Laurel to her feet, Jessica's teasing voice reached them again. "Come on — answer me, you two."

Ivan released Laurel's fingers. He motioned for her to follow him out of the room. Her eyes smarted. She had wanted to linger with Ivan, the two of them together beside the sleeping baby, listening to the sound of rain needling against the window. But Jessica had ruined everything.

The next thing Laurel knew, they were a trio again, seated at a low table in front of the fireplace fitting pieces into a large jigsaw puzzle. It was a pastoral scene with a farm and fields. As Jessica and Ivan sipped mugs of hot coffee, they worked on the cows while Laurel struggled with the undifferentiated pieces of blue sky.

"Nice place," Jessica mused, tapping a piece into place with her fingertips. "The weather's a lot better there than it is here."

Laurel glanced up. It looked gray-black outside. In the last half hour, the storm had increased in fury. Pine boughs scraped against the roof, wind made the house creak, and sheets of rain coated the western windows.

Ivan sighed contentedly. He flung one arm out along the edge of the couch. "I like a good storm. This beats tapping a gouge against wood."

"Mmmm . . ." Jessica agreed, purring like a cat. She leaned back against the couch. She closed her eyes. Pursed her lips. Her shoulder, Laurel noted, was very close to the tips of Ivan's fingers.

Jessica's eyes opened. Watching her, watching Ivan, made Laurel feel tense. Then, as if Ivan had read Laurel's mind, he drew his arm away and put both hands back on top of the table. "I think, given half a chance, I could get used to a life of leisure. Do you have popcorn? Maybe we can pop some later. What a life. No cares. Sitting cross-legged on this carpet, I feel like Bluebeard with my harem. Every man should be surrounded by women."

"Harem?" Jessica chuckled. "Say something, Pokey. This man is talking like a sexist, and we're not going to let him get away with it, are we?"

Laurel licked her lips. Her sister was joking, of course. But Jessica expected her to speak. She would have liked to defend Ivan, yet she couldn't. Ivan's harem. Who were they? Doe, Laurel, Jessica, and — of course — Allison, too, because Allison was everywhere. All of them? Laurel didn't want to be part of a harem, because she didn't want to share Ivan with anyone except Doe.

"Lau-rel?" Jessica tapped her shoulder playfully. "Has the cat got your tongue? Give this hirsute chauvinist a piece of your mind. Shall we expose him to the mercy of the elements? We don't have to put up with him, you know. We were doing fine, were perfectly happy playing our own game of chess before he appeared."

Jessica's face was animated. The glow from the fire made her cheeks as rosy as her jumpsuit. Laurel glanced at Ivan. But appearing to be oblivious to Jessica's beauty, his fingers danced over the puzzle. "It's been a while. Maybe I should check on Doe," he murmured.

"I'll do it," Laurel offered, anxious to put an end to this particular conversation.

Ivan shook his head. "No, don't jump up, butterfly. I'll go."

When he was pulling himself to his feet, someone pressed the buzzer at the kitchen door. The buzz was followed immediately by an impatient knocking and another staccato buzz.

Ivan frowned. "You're not expecting anyone, are you? Besides, who'd be outside in such foul weather?"

SIXTEEN

When Jessica opened the kitchen door, two nuns — one angular, one round — stepped in out of the rain. Their habits were wet and muddy. They were both shivering.

"I'm Sister Margaret and this is Sister Inez," the thin one said, tugging at the rosary hanging from her sash. "We're sorry to bother you, but we need to call the gas station."

"Maybe we can do something," Jessica offered.

Before either of the nuns could answer, Ivan stepped forward. "If it's your car, I can help."

Sister Margaret shook her head. "No, I wouldn't trouble you. It's just that, driving back from church, we've had a little mishap. I'll call the Harrison boy. It's just something silly with our Honda, so don't bother about us."

"It's no bother," Ivan insisted. "I'd be happy to take a look."

"I'll come, too," Laurel offered, eager to help with anything that Ivan was willing to do.

Sister Inez adjusted her wimple. "Sister Margaret," she said, "is embarrassed to admit that we've gotten the car stuck in a ditch."

"Well, that's easy enough," Ivan declared. "I can give you a push."

"I'm strong. I can push, too," Laurel said.

Ivan looked at Jessica. Then he turned toward her. "You might be as strong, muffin, but — if we need it — Jessica can drive."

"You don't need a driver," Sister Margaret declared. "Because I can do that. . . ."

Laurel pointed at her sister's velour jumpsuit. "Jessica would have to change, too. So it's settled. I'll come along, and she can stay with the baby."

"Oh, the baby," Sister Inez said, smiling at Ivan. "You're the father. A little girl, Annie says. We've seen her from a distance. But never close up. Maybe sometime. . . ."

A few minutes later, Laurel and Ivan, draped in slickers from the Tavrow tackle closet, followed the two nuns up the road to where their car was stuck. Ivan, carrying two fireplace logs, was humming. He didn't seem

to mind the rain. Laurel strode along next to
him. If he didn't care about the weather, she
didn't, either. Perhaps as they walked in the
rain, she'd have a chance to ask him about
her dream. She thought maybe the kite was
supposed to be Doe. Was it? And, if so, was
Allison really giving Doe to *her*?

Drops splattered noisily about them. Gusts
of wind fanned out through the woods, flat-
tening rye grass and aspen seedlings. The
gravel road was awash with muddy water.
Its potholes were miniature lakes filled with
pine needles. The ditches on either side looked
like bubbling brown creeks.

Laurel, enjoying herself, was in no hurry
to reach the car. But soon they found it angled
precariously, its rear wheels half submerged
in one of the ditches. When Ivan had assessed
the situation, he urged Sister Inez to take
shelter under a tree. Then he asked Sister
Margaret to get behind the wheel and wait
for further instructions.

"When they start the car, we'll push," Ivan
told Laurel, as they bent and wedged the logs
into the ditch. "If this doesn't work, we can
bring the truck."

Laurel nodded. "Just tell me what to do,"
she said. Although her feet were wet and
numb from the cold, the rest of her was dry.
She was glad to be out of the house. " 'The

rain is raining all around . . .' " she said.

Ivan flashed a grin in her direction. " 'Into each life some rain must fall' or even 'For the rain it raineth every day.' But now, instead of words, we must have action."

He cupped his hands around his mouth. "Sister Margaret . . . turn on the motor and put the car into drive. Next, *slowly* — slowly and evenly — put your foot on the pedal, and we'll be back here pushing."

"Now for the dirty work," he said, moving down into the ditch. Imitating him, Laurel stepped off the road.

"Oooh," she gasped, as she found herself in water up to her knees.

"Cold, I know," Ivan agreed sympathetically. "But I don't think this will take long. The real traction should come, not from us pushing, but from the placement of the logs."

The Honda vibrated, throbbing as its motor revved up. Laurel and Ivan stood side by side behind it.

"Now lean into it," he told her. "Yes . . . push and push. Okay, Sister, now. Take it from park into drive. Easy — don't panic. Just a little more gas. Yes — go for it."

The car's rear wheels churned up water. "Easy, easy," he shouted forward. "And for us," he told Laurel, "we'll place ourselves back here." Laurel didn't feel as if she was doing anything as she leaned her weight against the trunk of the car. For a moment, nothing happened.

Then the car lurched forward. Relieved, Laurel expected it to roll up onto the road. She braced her feet and pressed with her shoulder. Suddenly, however, she felt Ivan yanking her to one side. As he did, the car slipped backward into the spot where they had been standing. Dazed, Laurel breathed shallowly. If Ivan hadn't been alert, the car could have knocked them off their feet. Or worse.

She clutched her arms across her chest. She didn't want to come unglued, but she could feel herself start to shake.

"Cut — no wait. Sit tight," Ivan yelled up to Sister Margaret.

"Are you all right?" Sister Inez called out. "Don't you want my help, too?"

Ivan shook his head. "No, stay where you are. We're fine. See?" he said, turning back toward Laurel. "You're okay, aren't you? That was close, but not as bad as it seemed. Look at that right rear wheel. Now it's resting firmly on the logs we put there. Next time will be a cinch. And next time, we'll be at one side."

"I'm fine," she mumbled. "Fine, really I am. Don't worry."

"Are you sure?"

"I'm sure."

"Good girl," Ivan said soothingly. "I can always count on you." Then, motioning to indicate that Sister Inez should stay where she was, he jogged forward to give a new set of instructions to Sister Margaret.

A moment later, back by Laurel's side, he readjusted one of the logs. "Ah, that's better. That was a little dicey, scary, I know. But it wasn't and isn't a tragedy. The second time will be the charm. You'll see. We are a team, Laurel Tavrow."

Encouraged, Laurel obeyed his instructions. She stood by the fender. "Now," Ivan shouted to Margaret. "Yes, but more!" He clenched his teeth together. Imitating him, Laurel did the same. Together they pushed. For a moment, the right rear wheel bobbed up, but then it dipped down again. "Shoulder it — yes, once more should do it, baby," Ivan promised. And he was right. As they strained, the car's right rear wheel rolled up over the logs and spun onto the wet gravel.

"Stand back," Ivan told Laurel. "Enough, cut it," he shouted ahead. "Now wait. Sister Inez, go on — get in now."

As Ivan spoke, he splattered forward, and Laurel — flicking a piece of wet hair back from her face — followed him. Ivan had done it. He was wonderful. She knew she was right when she pictured herself at his side. What had he said? That they were a team. Well, they were. And what had Jessica said about love? Like a tidal wave. Yes, like that. Laurel's feelings were strong and clear.

"Oh, many thanks," Sister Inez said, as she hurried to slide into the passenger side of the car. "If you get in, we'll drive you home."

Laurel held her breath. That wasn't what she wanted. She wanted, even in the rain, some time to be alone with Ivan.

"No, then you'd have to turn around," Ivan told Sister Inez. As he continued, Laurel exhaled. "Besides, it's only a short way. And we're wet already."

Sister Margaret leaned over toward them. "Well, thank you, then. Thank you so much. And if there's ever anything we can do for you, let us know."

As the Honda headed slowly up the road, Ivan turned to her. "Come on," he said. "Let's go home."

Laurel fell into step beside him. Their shoulders kept bumping, but no matter how hard she willed it, Ivan didn't throw an arm around her or take her hand. Instead, like a child, he stomped into every puddle. "Wet is wet," he declared.

"Ivan . . ." she said, trying to decide whether to ask about her dream or about something even more important.

"Hmm? Hey, don't slow up. The object of the game is to get back so we can take hot showers. Come on." He took her elbow and nudged her forward.

Laurel stopped. "Ivan?"

"What?"

"Ivan?" she repeated, hesistantly.

"What? Out with it," he said.

"Do you love me?"

Ivan's hand dropped to his side. "Of course, I do," he said, without skipping a beat. "As I love Doe, as I love all my friends, my friend. . . ."

Friend? The word cut into her. "But, Ivan — Ivan, I — "

"You what?" Ivan planted himself in front of her, lifted her chin with his fingers. "Oh, no, honey, no. I thought that was a phase. I thought it had passed. I mean — look, Laurel, I love you. I do. But there's love, and there's love. And besides, I don't rob cradles."

Blinking, she shoved his hand away from her chin. She pulled her hood forward and jerked to one side so he couldn't examine her face now that it was streaked with both rain and tears. Had she heard him right? Had he really said, "I don't rob cradles"?

"But, Ivan — " she pleaded. By now she was beyond feeling pride or putting up a good front. "It can't be this way. You'll change. Things will be different. You'll see. After Jessica leaves, we can — Oh, listen, Ivan, I'll — "

"Enough!" he said. "Come on. You've gotten carried away. You're hallucinating. Imagining things. Pretend this never happened, and that it's only a bad dream. Let time pass. Time will make a difference. Shhhh! Hush, now. Come on — step it up. Let's go. Let's get on with it. You need a hot shower, cocoa, a fire. So, march!"

Who was he talking to? To her? To Doe? Laurel was imagining things. Ivan wasn't speaking to *her*. When she closed her eyes, she could picture him lecturing Allison. Then that image dissolved and was replaced by one of Allison flying the kite, handing it to Laurel. Poor Allison, why should she have to give up the beautiful kite?

Laurel opened her eyes. Her head felt weightless, disconnected from her body. "This is not happening," she told herself. The storm had confused her. It was too windy to understand what anyone was saying. Ivan started to walk. She hopped forward, anxious to catch up to him. A moment later he began to run. She ran after him. Yes, she had imagined everything. Ivan was right. She needed a shower, hot chocolate, a crackling fire. She also needed time and another chance.

SEVENTEEN

AUGUST

August was slipping by. While Laurel watched, Doe prowled around the edges of the playpen. Frowning, the child examined the bars of her prison, as if she was searching for some way to escape.

Oblivious to his daughter, Ivan leaned against the porch of the cabin. He had a tablet in his hands. He was sketching. "Put your arms out," he said. "Further. Stretch them. That's right — yes. Hold it."

His words were addressed to Jessica. Laurel stood beneath a pine tree observing. As she looked at Ivan and her sister, she attempted to block out what Ivan had said in the rain. Then, twisting her hands together, she wondered how Jessica had managed to get to the cabin ahead of her. When she left the house, she had assumed that Jessica was asleep. She had been mistaken, for poised atop the stump, as though it were a pedestal, was her sister.

Dressed in a shiny white leotard, her skin pale, Jessica seemed like a statue come to life. Although Laurel was in the shade, she felt hot. She wanted to scream at Ivan. At her sister, too. But she didn't. Instead, she bit down on her lower lip.

Every few minutes, Ivan gave another series of commands, and Jessica changed her position. Doe continued to circle the playpen, but no one paid any attention to her.

Ivan's hands moved rapidly. He was absorbed in what he was doing. He was making drawings of Jessica, of Jessica's body. All the lines were rounded as Jessica was rounded. Laurel could imagine the luscious, curving sculpture that Ivan would carve.

Jessica didn't seem impressed that Ivan was drawing her. Although she obeyed his commands, she laughed at them. Her body was motionless, but her mouth rattled on, describing an apartment design which had individual living quarters but a common kitchen and dining area.

"That way people have both privacy and community at the same time," she explained. "I think it's a way to combat anomie — the isolation that people complain of. What do you think? Would you like to live that way?"

Ivan nodded. "Sit cross-legged. Yes — like that — perfect. Yes, I like the concept. Think how it would be for Doe and me. A sharing arrangement would offer her the people contact she needs. It's not good for her to be alone with me all the time. Then, of course, I'd have to have my studio somewhere else."

"That would be better," Jessica said. "She wouldn't be in your hair all the time. If she had more company, maybe she'd be friendlier, too. Then, of course, it would be easy to find someone to look after her."

Laurel wrapped her arms around the tree. Two weeks ago she would have leaped forward to say that Ivan didn't need anyone to look after Doe because she was there and she intended to stay with them. Because she and Ivan were in love with each other. Now she was no longer sure of how he felt. Or of how she felt.

Yes, she continued to baby-sit for Doe. But Jessica was there, too, lounging about, talking with Ivan. Ivan didn't shut Laurel out or forget to smile and compliment her. He did, however, accept Jessica's presence happily. The three of them swam together, cooked meals, took walks. Though Laurel tried to swallow her jealousy, she couldn't seem to do it.

Even the fact that Jessica was leaving did

not console Laurel, because it wasn't only Jessica that was bothering her. Allison continued to hover nearby. Laurel saw her as the woman in her dream, looking like Ivan's sculpture — a slim redhead with a sad mouth. When Laurel gazed at the carving, she felt that Doe's mother was watching her with unblinking eyes and empty arms.

Jessica had complained that the sculpture gave her goose bumps. So now, Laurel noticed, the figure was covered with a dropcloth. But still, Allison was there as part of Ivan's harem. Or as part of Laurel's dream. Several times a day, the dream washed over her with such vividness that it seemed to be happening again.

Slowly, Laurel had begun to feel close to Allison, sympathetic. She could see the kite, which *had* to be Doe, with its beauty muted, faded as Allison entrusted it to her. What was wrong? Why had the iridescence faded? What was Laurel supposed to understand or to do? There was a mystery to Allison, to Doe, to the whole dream that she could not unravel.

A voice cut into Laurel's reverie. "Be-be-be," Doe said impatiently as she reached toward Ivan.

Laurel forced herself back into the present. She looked past Doe to the shrouded sculpture, to Ivan and Jessica, who were deep in conversation. That was real. The dream had seemed real, too. But what about the conversation in the rain? Had Ivan actually said, "I don't rob cradles," or because Laurel was wet, cold, and tired, had she imagined it?

Questions and more questions. Questions, not just about Doe or Allison, but about Jessica, too. Laurel needed advice — the kind of advice that a mother was supposed to give. If Ivan loved Laurel, why didn't he resent anyone who came between them? Sometimes she told herself that when Jessica left everything would be the same.

Laurel remembered how Ivan had behaved toward Miles. He seemed to be doing the same thing with her sister. Jessica couldn't be alarmed that she spent her time there if Jessica liked Ivan. That was what Laurel thought in the good moments. In the bad ones, she decided that Ivan and Jessica were falling in love.

While Laurel was debating these matters, Doe caught sight of her. Swaying back and forth, the child began to shriek emphatically. Pleased at the unexpected burst of recognition, Laurel trotted forward and lifted Doe into her arms.

Ivan smiled and waved. "I know someone who's awfully glad to see you," he said.

Laurel held the baby away from her chest. Doe pulled at Laurel's nose and wrinkled up her own. Perhaps Ivan was right. Perhaps, Doe — in her own solid, sober way — was pleased to see her. "Doe's happy to see me, but what about you?" Laurel wanted to ask Ivan. "What about you?"

Jessica blew a kiss in Laurel's direction. "Good morning, sleepyhead," she said. "Since it's my last day, I decided not to waste it."

Doe reached toward Ivan's pad and pencil. "Be-be-be," she said, struggling to free herself from Laurel's arms.

"Laurel," Ivan groaned. "I hate to ask, but could you pull her away?"

"Sure," she answered.

Ivan winked. "Good. Thanks. You see, I'm determined to finish these sketches before Jessica goes."

"Be-be-be-be," Doe protested, swatting at Laurel. Then she scrunched up her face and started to wail.

Ivan swiveled his head in their direction. "Don't just stand there. Do something," he urged Laurel. "Play games, amuse her. Something . . . *anything*."

Laurel bounced Doe up and down. As the child grew calmer, Laurel noticed something. She sniffed and poked one hand in the leg of the diaper to see if the baby needed changing. She did. Ivan had probably known that all along, been waiting for Laurel to appear and tackle the dirty job.

"Is she all right?" he asked.

"She's fine," Laurel replied, trying not to look annoyed. "And don't worry, I'll take Doe on a picnic. I'll give you time. All the time you want."

She tried to sound casual, contented to go off and leave them alone. She did not want to acknowledge the burning sensation in the bottom of her stomach. Never had Laurel wanted anything as much as she had wanted to make Ivan and Doe a permanent part of her life. Without Jessica. And even if Laurel felt strangely sympathetic toward her, without Allison, either. Suddenly, against her will, she could — once again — see herself cradling the frayed, silent kite in her arms.

"Forget Allison," she told herself brusquely.

A dream, after all, was only a dream, as a day was just a day. All she had to get through was one more day before Jessie was gone. She could do that. She knew she could. One thing at a time.

As Laurel picked her way through the woods, she sang nursery rhymes. She hoped that the sound of her voice would amuse Doe and chase away disturbing thoughts. Doe seemed happy, but Laurel's spirits didn't improve. She wondered how Jessica and Ivan had managed to get rid of her so easily. If Ivan's behavior bewildered her, her sister's did, too. Why did Jessica have to come and cause trouble for Laurel?

As Laurel asked herself this unanswerable question, she turned off the trail and began to follow the wide swath of a fire lane. Behind the woodpecker tree, distinguished by its pockmarked trunk, she turned into the hidden meadow. No one, except for Spencer, knew this spot existed. As children, they had picnicked there whenever they wanted to be alone. It was a warm, dry place that had few flies or mosquitoes.

Before Laurel took Doe off her back, she checked to make sure the meadow had no poison ivy. She picked up twigs and sharp stones and flung them into the woods. When she was satisfied, she reached back to lift the baby from the carrier.

Then Laurel unpacked a ball and a box of miniature alphabet blocks. She tried to interest Doe in a game with the ball; but the child, pushing it aside impatiently, crawled around in circles, examining the grass and the late-summer wildflowers.

Laurel leaned against a log. It occurred to her that Doe had probably never been in deep grass. Around the cabin, there was mostly sand. Other places, she and Ivan held her, spent so much time keeping her away from danger that she never had a chance to experiment. Eyes alert and staring, Doe plucked at the grass. She sniffed at it. Tentatively, she fingered some bluebells. Her hand moved over them as though they might disappear if she wasn't careful.

"Ba-ba?" she asked, glancing back at Laurel.

A minute later, losing interest, she crawled forward again. When Doe stopped to poke at a caterpillar, Laurel rocked back on her heels. When Doe started to crawl again, Laurel dropped onto her hands and knees.

"Crawling is fun," she told the child. "No wonder you don't want to walk. But still, there's something different about you. Spencer sees it. And in my dream, for a moment, I saw it. . . ."

As Doe scrambled off, Laurel followed. She reached with her hands and pushed with her knees, imitating the way the baby moved. Laurel tried to pretend that she wasn't imitating Doe but that she *was* Doe. Maybe then she'd understand. She felt the grass cool and damp beneath her. It was soft. It smelled delicious. No wonder Doe had sniffed appreciatively. Tiny red-brown ants crawled along between strands of grass. A monarch butterfly fluttered over a milkweed vine, but when Laurel reached out, it soared away.

EIGHTEEN

A rabbit appeared at the edge of the clearing. He flattened his ears against his head. His nose pulsed. Laurel wiggled her nose, too. Doe dropped onto her stomach and stared at the brown-furred creature. Laurel copied her. Doe looked frightened. So did the rabbit.

Each seemed frozen to the spot. Laurel tried to examine the rabbit as if she'd never seen one before either, as if it were as large in proportion to her body as it was in proportion to Doe's. She could see that the fur lightened at the tips of the ears, that there were veins on the inside. Did Doe see those things, too? Did Doe know that the rabbit was shy? Or did she think he was dangerous?

Finally, Doe lurched forward and headed toward the rabbit. In a second, the creature sprang out of sight. Grunting, Doe headed off in another direction. Laurel followed her.

In and out of shadow they crawled, tunneling mazes through the grass. As Laurel padded along, she felt younger and younger. Doe stopped to taste a flower, so she tasted one. When Doe spit hers out, she did the same. When Doe pointed at a hawk whose shadow dusted over them, Laurel stuck a finger into the air. Soon Laurel was in a quiet green world of touch, taste, and smell.

If she couldn't be completely grown-up, being a baby was easy, she decided. Easier than being in love and hurting inside. Being a baby was lovely. She felt free. She was thinking like Doe, forgetting the world beyond the meadow. And yet, somewhere in the back of her head, something nagged at her. She knew she had never been a baby like Doe. Doe was splendid, like the kite shimmering silently in the sky, but she *was* different.

Laurel was still trying to figure out how the child was different when Doe turned and began to chase after her. She uttered triumphant high-pitched sounds each time she was able to close her fingers over Laurel's toes. "What a baby you are," Laurel told her. "And what about me? What would your daddy and Jessica say if they could see me now?"

"Be-be," Doe answered.

"Right. That's right. They'd tell me I'm nothing but a baby. And maybe I am, but...."

Laurel let her voice trail off. It was upsetting to have Jessica and Ivan creep into her thoughts again, making her feel discontented. She rolled onto her back. Doe crawled over and climbed up onto her stomach. Laurel bounced her there. "Well, look at you. Since when do you like me this much? Since when, huh?"

Doe's mouth curved into a smile as Laurel held her up overhead. "Do you love me? Do you? Then throw kisses or laugh or do something." Laurel propped the baby on her knees and jiggled her. "No giggles, huh? Did you giggle for your mother? Did you? Is Spencer right when he says you're strange? Maybe . . . maybe so, but you're not retarded. Only quiet and serious. I'd be serious, too, if I had only a father to look after me. You need a mommy and a daddy, don't you, Doe-baby?"

When Laurel got no response to her questions, she swung Doe over to one side and put her down in the grass. "If you can't talk to me, then I'm just going to let you be," Laurel told her sternly.

Doe didn't seem to mind. She pivoted on her knees and veered off again. Laurel shifted to her stomach. Lazily, she squinted after the child. What was it, Laurel kept asking, that made Doe so different? If she could only, for once, figure it out.

A squadron of army jets droned through the sky. "Planes," she told Doe. "Look at the airplanes." Doe didn't show any interest in the jets. Well, maybe the child was right, why should she look after planes when the meadow teemed with entrancing things?

Laurel wondered what Ivan and Jessica were doing, what time it was. Though she meant to focus her attention on the baby, she kept seeing her sister and Ivan. They were swimming. They were canoeing. Laughing. Touching.

"No," she shouted, suddenly alert. "No, Doe! Don't touch. No — no — no! Hot. Do you hear me? No!"

Slowly, deliberately, the baby was closing her fingers over a large wasp. She squeezed it intently.

"No!" Laurel shouted. "Hot! No! No!"

Doe paid no attention to Laurel's voice. She didn't turn or look up. Then, a second later, Laurel's cries and Doe's mingled, rising out of the grass. As the baby wailed, Laurel did, too. Doe hadn't even blinked when Laurel warned her of danger. Oblivious, she had crushed the wasp in her palm. Now she was wailing because she had been stung. But Laurel's anguished cry came from another source.

Suddenly she knew what the problem was.

She knew why Doe was different; why she often seemed remote, removed. Doe, like the dream kite, existed in a world of silence. She hadn't heard Laurel's warning. Because Doe could not hear. She could not hear a thing.

With the baby held close to her chest, Laurel plunged from the meadow, down the fire trail, and back toward the cabin.

"Ivan, Ivan," she cried as she approached. Then she screamed louder, trying to make her voice heard over the baby's wails. *"I-van!"*

"What is it? What?" he called, running from the cabin.

Laurel felt weak-kneed, out of control. "She's deaf, Ivan — she can't hear. Deaf . . . deaf. That's why the wasp stung her hand. Because she couldn't *hear* me, couldn't hear me calling. Or the airplane. Deaf . . . she's deaf."

"A wasp? Where?" Ivan grabbed for the baby. Then he pried at one of her tightly clenched fists.

"No — the left, the other one. But, Ivan, she's deaf. She can't *hear*."

"What kind of wasp?" Ivan asked. "What did it look like? There, Doe-baby, there. It's going to be all right, honey girl, all right. That's it — yes. Hey, Laurel, wake up! We need a book!"

For a moment Laurel was transfixed. "But, Ivan," she protested, wondering if Doe's howls had blocked half her words. "It's not just the wasp. She's deaf. Your daughter is deaf."

Ivan reached out and gave Laurel a push. "Look up 'Bites and Stings.'"

Doe continued to cry. Seeing her father had not comforted her. Ivan didn't seem to understand what Laurel was saying. Frightened, she turned toward the cabin.

Jessica was standing in the doorway. "Come get this ice," she called, holding up a plastic bag filled with cubes. "And I'll go make a paste with baking soda."

Almost mechanically, Laurel took the ice and sat next to Ivan on the stump. She helped press it against Doe's palm. The three of them seated close together on the stump — Ivan, Laurel, and Doe. Ivan rocked the baby. He sang to her, kissed her, as Laurel slid the plastic-wrapped cubes back and forth across her hand.

After a while, Doe's cries subsided into a series of hiccuping sobs. Ivan's shoulder was touching Laurel's. She could feel the warmth of his legs. Trying to contain the fluttery feeling in her stomach, she looked down. This wasn't the time to worry about Doe's hearing. First, they had to take care of her and make sure she was not in pain. Laurel thought she should get more ice, yet she didn't move. Everything seemed to be slowed down, filtered through layers of fog.

In some hazy way, though, another matter — aside from Doe's deafness — was bothering her. It revolved around Ivan. Ivan and Jessica and Ivan's cutoffs. He'd had on something else when she'd left. And Jessie — Jessie, a moment ago, had stood in the doorway wrapped in a towel. Only a towel. So, they'd been swimming. Swimming. She and Ivan had been swimming, too. And yet. . . .

"Shush . . . hush. Easy, baby . . . easy," Ivan urged his daughter.

Laurel moved the ice in a circular motion across the baby's palm. She peered at the raised, swollen bump. Then when she looked up she saw Jessica approaching. Jessica was wearing her leotard with white shorts on over it. It was dry. Her hair was dry.

Jessica took Doe's hand and began to smear a thick white paste on it. "This is what Mom always did for us," she said.

Laurel flinched. Frowning at her sister, she edged away from Ivan. Her head throbbed as if it were being tapped with a dozen of Ivan's mallets. She was imagining things, making them up, exaggerating. Jessica hadn't been in a towel. Doe's screaming had confused her. Jessica was fine. She looked like Jessica. She was dressed like Jessica. And, as for Ivan, she couldn't seem to remember what he'd worn earlier.

Laurel stood up. She backed away. Ivan was sitting on the stump with Doe in his lap as Jessica knelt next to them tending the baby's hand. Father, baby, mother. Well, where did that leave her? Where did it leave Allison?

Forcing herself back into the present, she spoke. "We've got to help Doe," she said.

Ivan and Jessica turned to look at her.

"But we have," Ivan told her.

"No, no, we haven't," Laurel insisted. "She's deaf. I told you before, but you didn't hear me. She's deaf, Ivan. She can't hear. That's what's different about her. That's — "

Doe whimpered. Ivan cuddled her affectionately against his chest. "You're wrong," he said, speaking in a soft, self-controlled voice. "You got panicky, honey. You just lost your cool, that's all."

Jessica sat cross-legged at Ivan's feet. "Oh, Pokey, it's the same old thing. You always get carried away."

For a moment, Laurel gritted her teeth. Then she spoke again. "But I didn't. Doe can't hear. Look at her. I can stand and shout, but she won't even turn her head." Laurel let her voice get louder and louder. Unresponsive, Doe nestled against Ivan.

"Quiet! Easy there," Ivan growled. "I've just gotten her calmed down. Now leave it. Leave it be. There's nothing wrong with Doe. Nothing."

Laurel jumped to her feet. "Let's do a test."

Ivan shook his head. "Let's not."

Jessica sent a meaningful look in Laurel's direction. "Don't ruin my last day here. Now ease up, will you? She's not your kid."

Laurel stared at Ivan, at Doe, at Jessica. Ivan was not acting the way he should. He wasn't even listening.

Laurel took a few steps backward. The sun was bright. A hot breeze was blowing off the lake. Its surface gleamed like wrinkled aluminum foil. She was perspiring heavily. She needed to cool off. Maybe instead of running through the woods, she'd swim home. Spencer was in the next cove tinkering with his boat. He'd listen to her. He knew there was something strange about Ivan, unusual about Doe.

"You saw her with the pots and pans. She blinked when you banged them together," Ivan said.

"And when she banged on Spencer's piano," Laurel told herself, remembering. And yet why not test Doe? Something *was* wrong with her. Ivan and Jessica turned away from

Laurel. They exchanged a private look.

"Doe," Laurel called. "Doe, Doe, Doe-baby! DOE! DOE!"

Laurel whistled. She bellowed. She cawed like a crow. Then when she fell silent, she heard Allison's voice crooning, and she started calling again. "DOE! DOE! DOE!" But Doe didn't move. She didn't turn. She didn't blink.

Distraught, Laurel turned away and ran down the path toward the lake.

NINETEEN

Thoughtfully, Laurel walked along the beach.
It was August fourteenth. Jessica was gone,
and Miles wouldn't be back until midnight.
Tomorrow Miles would want her to stay at
home to celebrate her birthday with him. If
she hoped to put her plan into action, this was
her only chance.

The sand beneath her feet was pockmarked
from an early evening rain. She tried to make
herself weightless so that she wouldn't leave
footprints. This was a game she'd played
when she was a child. It hadn't worked then,
and it didn't work now. She sighed.

Ivan was in the canoe, steering it along
the weedy edge of the sandbar, gliding in and
out of the fading pools of light. Doe wasn't
with him. Though he'd promised Laurel that
he'd never leave the baby alone in the cabin
again, Jessica had bewitched him. Before

she'd come, everything had been perfect. Laurel kicked at a clod of sand. Her toe hit a stone.

"Ouch," she said.

Laurel had to make a decision, and she didn't have much time. She could fight, win Ivan back. Or she could stage a different kind of fight. A fight for Doe. Laurel didn't know if Doe could hear or not, but she was determined to find out. She couldn't go back to baby-sitting for Ivan, pretending nothing had happened in the last two weeks. Shadows clouded her mind and voices echoed there, too. Jessica and Ivan. *I don't rob cradles.* Doe crushing a wasp in her hand. *Oh, Pokey, you always get carried away.* A silent dream-kite.

Laurel couldn't forget any of them, especially the notion that Doe could not hear. Why had Ivan refused to listen? How would Allison feel if she thought her baby was deaf? If Laurel had a baby, she would be a good mother. She'd pay close attention, want to know if her baby was deaf. So would Allison, she decided. But Ivan didn't. His stubbornness was goading her.

She'd brooded about that all day. When Jessica had gone to say goodbye to Ivan, she'd stayed behind, lying moodily on her bed. Now, still brooding, she looked out at Ivan drifting in the canoe. Had he spotted her on the beach?

Maybe. But she had something important to do. Resolutely she walked on toward the cabin.

As she passed the Harrison dock, she glanced at the rowboat, at the green canvas tarp lying next to it on the beach. Just when she was wondering why the tarp was off the boat, she stumbled and fell.

"Gotcha!" a fiendish voice rumbled. "So, now that the luscious Jessica has gone, the luscious Laurel is going to reclaim her one true sweetheart. Ain't love grand?"

Turning her head, she watched as Spencer crawled from under the green canvas. He'd hidden himself there for no other purpose than to reach out and trip her.

"Creep, despicable creep," she muttered.

She wanted to yell, to get back at Spencer for his smart mouth and childish pranks. But as she was going to let him have it, something occurred to her. If she put her plan into action, she'd need him.

She raised herself to her elbows and watched as he lifted the tarp and began tying it around the rowboat. "Spence?"

He glanced at her suspiciously. "What?"

"You working tonight?" She tried to sound casual, but she knew she hadn't fooled him.

"Yes. Why? Oh, I got it — you want me to take you and Ivan to the drive-in. What's the matter with the back of his truck?"

"Shut up, Spencer."

Spencer wound a rope around a metal cleat. "What do you want?"

Laurel scanned the lake. It was getting dark, but Ivan remained out there paddling noiselessly. Was he listening to their words drift out over the water? "Mmm . . . I do want something," she admitted, turning back toward Spencer.

"Like what?"

She dropped her voice until it was barely more than a whisper. "A lift in your car."

Spencer frowned, but when he spoke his voice was as muted as hers. "How can I give you a lift if I'm working?"

"You can if you want. Get your mom to cover for you. Or Billy."

"Anything to do with Ivan?"

"Maybe."

"Why are we whispering, Pokey? What's going on? What's the mystery?"

"I can't tell you now. But I'll find you. At the station. In a while. Okay? But don't tell anyone about this — promise?"

Spencer grinned at her. She thought he was going to turn her down, but he didn't. "I promise," he agreed at last. "You won't be long, will you?"

Laurel didn't answer him. Instead, she

turned and stepped into the grass at the edge of the sand. It rustled and tickled her arms. As she walked, mosquitoes rose up in clouds, buzzing, stinging. Impatiently she brushed them off.

Ivan was motionless now, and he was far away. Even if he came to shore at full speed, it would take him five or ten minutes. Besides, he didn't look as though he was about to turn back. He was bent forward. He seemed to be brooding. Was he worrying about his daughter? Did he care that Laurel hadn't come to baby-sit? Did he miss Jessica?

Trying to move as quietly as possible, Laurel approached the cabin. She trembled as she edged around toward the back door. The sound of her breathing seemed loud and raspy. When she stepped in, the floor creaked.

"Doe?" she whispered. "Doe?"

When Laurel stepped forward, the floor creaked again. Doe didn't stir. Laurel leaned forward so she could peer outside. Ivan was drifting in the rapidly fading light. Moving back from the window, Laurel approached the crib.

"Doe," she said. "Doe, do you hear me? It's me, Laurel. Hey, Doe-baby?"

Laurel leaned on the crib railing and stared at the child. She tried to match her breathing with Doe's, but the baby breathed much faster. Laurel snapped her fingers. Then she did it again and again. Doe slept on. Laurel clapped her hands together. Nothing. Nothing at all.

For a moment, she scanned the cabin. When she looked down at Doe, the baby's eyes were open. She rolled onto her back and gazed solemnly at Laurel. Laurel shivered. Maybe the clapping *had* awakened her.

"Be-be," Doe murmured sleepily. She reached out in Laurel's direction. "Be-be-be-be."

The child's voice had a monotone quality Laurel had never noticed before. As Laurel watched, Doe began to pull herself to her feet. "Be-be," she repeated, and — in a shy, sweet way — she smiled.

Laurel didn't move. Trying to make a decision, she studied the baby. Was she being brave or stupid? Was Ivan still on the lake? Or was he lurking outside ready to pounce on her and ask what she thought she was doing there?

Suddenly Laurel made up her mind. She grabbed for the blanket that was tossed over the end of the crib. Moving quickly, she lowered the side of the crib and tucked the blanket around Doe. Doe's arms stretched up. Laurel leaned over and took hold of her.

"Come on," she breathed. "Come on, baby. We're getting out of here. But I'm doing this for *you* — because you need help."

Then, without pausing to reconsider, Laurel turned and fled from the cabin. Taking first one trail and then another, she hurried as fast as she could. Doe was a dead weight in her arms. Laurel wished she'd thought to bring the carrier, but it was too late now.

She veered away from the water and made her way through the woods. Doe's head wobbled groggily against Laurel's shoulder. From time to time, Laurel — wondering if Ivan had come in from the lake — stopped to listen for footsteps. All she heard, however, were bats squealing and careening through the trees.

She knew what she was doing. She was going to get help. Trying to hurry, she skirted the Harrison house, headed down the dirt road which led out to the highway. Though her route was a familiar one, she felt lonely, unprotected.

Trees, tall and straight, swayed around her, watching her flee. King Tarik. Queen Ingrid. The whole Druid court. There was something unreal about stumbling along a rutted road in the dark cradling a sleeping child to her chest. Maybe this wasn't happening but was a nightmare. Maybe if she stretched, she'd wake up and find she was dreaming.

She was lightheaded. She'd snatched a baby from her crib. Though she was a criminal, a thief, she was not going to turn back. She would follow this eerie waking dream on to its conclusion.

"One foot, other foot," she told herself encouragingly. "Keep going. Just keep going."

Then from behind her, lights flickered, wheels crunched into the graveled surface of the road. Laurel jumped back and crouched behind a clump of young aspens. Their leaves spun as the car slid by. It wasn't Ivan's truck. It was a station wagon from the peeled-bark lodge. Some of the nuns on their way to a movie, she decided.

Swatting mosquitoes, she stepped back into the road. The cloud of dust made her cough. Off to one side, she heard crackling and recognized the unmistakable sound of footsteps in the underbrush. Clutching Doe tightly, Laurel stopped. She listened. In the shadows, someone was watching her. Laurel wanted to turn and run, but with the baby in her arms she would never escape.

After what seemed like an endless time, she heard steps again. This time they were deliberate, careful. They were very close. Then, once again, they stopped. Trying to see into the darkness, Laurel scanned the woods.

No matter how hard she looked, she couldn't see anything. It was Ivan, playing a fiendish game, taking revenge on her for stealing his child. She felt as if she were a rubber band being stretched too thin. She hitched the baby higher, gripped her possessively. At last she couldn't stand it any longer.

"Cut it out," she cried. "Either take her or let me go. I know what's best for Doe. And for me — and it's not you!"

For a moment there was no response. Then, without warning, she heard a crash. What she saw, however, was not Ivan but a deer with a fawn. The two of them streaked across the road in front of her, vanishing as abruptly as they had appeared.

Laurel started to run. She'd been wrong. It hadn't been Ivan — just a pair of wild creatures who were as frightened as she was. But next time the threat might be real. This night, this baby, Laurel's flight were real. Dangerous and frightening. She had to move faster.

Trying not to stumble, she lurched down the dirt road like an overburdened horse. Despite stabbing pains in her side, she forced herself to keep going until, at last, she saw the circle of light.

"Spencer!" She hurtled forward with one last burst of speed. "Spencer!"

He ran to meet her. "What's going on?" he demanded, reaching out to take Doe. "Why do you have the baby?"

"Jane," Laurel panted. "Take us to Jane."

"Is she sick? Is this what you were talking about before? Or is it something else? Jane's not at the clinic now. It's too late. What *is* going on?"

Laurel shook her head impatiently. She didn't have enough breath to offer an explanation. "Please," she pleaded. "I need Jane — please!"

Spencer looked puzzled, but he responded to the urgency in her voice. Putting one hand in the small of her back, he guided her toward his car.

TWENTY

As Spencer and Laurel drove up, they could see Jane Collier through her kitchen window. She was sitting at the table eating lasagne out of a tinfoil container. Dressed in jeans and a plaid shirt, she did not look like a doctor. Nor did she appear much older than she had when she'd worked as summer help for the Tavrows. That comforted Laurel, but at the same time it made her uneasy.

Looking less startled than Laurel would have imagined, Jane responded to their knocking by shoving her newspaper aside. She opened the door and ushered them in, "What's up?" she asked.

Spencer spoke first. "The baby belongs to our tenant."

On the ride into town, Laurel had tried to compose herself, but as she came out of the darkness into the glare of the kitchen, she felt frightened again. "I wouldn't bother you now," she began. "I wouldn't, but there's something wrong with her. And it's important."

Jane cocked her head to one side. "Must be if you have to come here at nine-thirty at night. Spence, clear the papers away while I wash up. Laurel, undress the baby. Yes — use the table. Then we'll take a look."

Laurel watched Jane roll up her sleeves, scrub her hands. Then, deliberately, Laurel put Doe on the table, unfolded the blanket, stripped off the diaper and undershirt. Doe's eyes were open, but she seemed dazed and unresponsive. "Well . . ." Laurel said, aware that Jane expected her to explain why they were there.

"Come, come," Jane urged in a friendly yet businesslike tone. "I'm no mind reader. Where's the emergency? All I see is a sleepy female infant with nasty insect bites and some kind of food rash. Orange juice probably. Has she been checked for an orange juice allergy, do you know?"

Laurel shook her head. "No, but that's not it, though. It's something else. And her father won't listen. That's why *I* brought her here to have you tell me."

"So what is it?" Jane asked.

Laurel swallowed hard. "I think she's deaf."

Instead of commenting that possible deafness was not a nighttime emergency, Jane reached for the bag she had left by the back door. Then she took out her instruments and began to examine Doe. Doe watched the doctor with a drowsy version of her usual suspicious look.

As Jane poked and probed, Spencer leaned against the kitchen wall, scanning the Minneapolis paper. Laurel stood next to him. She wasn't interested in the news, but she glanced at it anyway.

Jane used her stethoscope, a tongue depressor. She thumped the baby's stomach, peered into her ears with a pointed instrument. As she worked, she made clucking noises. When Jane's routine survey was finished, she began a series of experiments.

She held Doe in a sitting position and thumped the table with a spoon. She tapped on a nearby chair. Next, holding Doe by the shoulders, she turned her so that the baby couldn't see her mouth. Then she tried a series of whistles.

Laurel watched silently. She didn't think she saw any response from the baby, but she wasn't sure. Doe seemed to be awake, but she reacted as if she heard neither the tapping nor the whistling.

After a while, Jane asked Spencer to open and close the door. He did. Doe blinked.

"Again," Jane said. "Half a dozen times. Yes."

Every time he slammed the door, Doe blinked and raised her arms convulsively.

"She hears that," Spencer said. "And at our place, she played the piano and liked it."

Jane frowned. "What else? Motorboats? Washing machines?"

Laurel had never paid close attention, but there was one thing she remembered immediately. "Pots and pans," she answered. "She bangs on them with a spoon."

"Mmm," Jane said. "Well . . . yes."

Spencer slammed the door again, shutting it so hard that everything in the kitchen jumped, including Doe.

"That's enough," Jane told him. Then she turned to Laurel. "Okay — go ahead, diaper her. Dress her."

"Her diaper is wet," Laurel murmured apologetically. "And I forgot to bring clean ones."

"Look in the hall closet," Jane told her. "I probably have samples. Just grab one."

"She's not deaf, is she?" Spencer asked.

Jane frowned. "Go ahead and dress her.

She's sleepy and should be in bed."

Laurel wanted an answer to Spencer's question, but she could see that Jane didn't intend to be rushed. Finally, as Laurel was dressing the baby, Jane spoke.

"It's hard to tell — on a child this young and in the middle of the night. The door slamming is never conclusive because of the amount of vibration. I need equipment. Another doctor to look at her."

Jane's eyes narrowed. She looked searchingly at Laurel. "But tell me something. Is this the sculptor's baby? And, if so, why did *you* bring her? And why sneak here at night instead of coming during clinic hours?"

"We didn't sneak," Spencer answered. "We drove up in my car."

"That's not what Jane means," Laurel said, rocking Doe in her arms. "I was sneaky. I brought her now because Ivan — her father — wouldn't listen to me, wouldn't even admit she might need testing."

Jane began putting her instruments back into her brown bag. "Not uncommon," she said. "It's fear. Parents deny because they are afraid of the truth. Well, forget that for now. Her father must be frantic. Telephone him."

"I can't. There's no phone."

"Then get into that car, and take her back

immediately. I'll come by late tomorrow, after clinic, and talk with him — see if I can't persuade him that more testing might be advisable."

Everything Jane said made sense. Laurel nodded. She was relieved that Jane had examined Doe and would check her again. But she was still upset. There was something beyond the subject of deafness that continued to disturb her. About Ivan. About Allison and why, if she was an alert, caring mother, she wasn't with her baby.

When Laurel thought of seeing Ivan face-to-face, she felt panicky. She was worried about herself and about the baby, but she didn't know how to explain this to Jane, so she didn't say anything except "Okay."

By the time Laurel and Doe were back in the VW with Spencer, she knew she couldn't possibly take Doe to Ivan. "Spence?"

"Huh?"

"What if you drop me and the baby at my house? Then you go tell him where we are."

Spencer guided the car around a wide S-curve in the road. "Him — you mean Ivan, huh? Why're you making me do the dirty work?"

Laurel's voice stuck in her throat. "I'm afraid," she said.

"It's about time. All night you've acted like stealing a kid is nothing. Well, finally big brave Laurel admits she's done something terrible. And I don't blame you for being spooked. I am, too. That guy's probably going to kill me, Pokey."

"Please, Spencer. Oh, please, please. . . ."

He nodded grimly. "Yeah, calm down. I'll do it. I don't know why, but I will. For you — anything. I must be out of my mind. But okay, yes, sure."

Relieved, Laurel settled back into the seat. Returning Doe was not going to be easy, but at least she had Spencer to help. Spencer did have a few good points. Maybe, if she were willing to try and talk to him, she could figure out what was bothering her.

"Spence — about Ivan?"

"What about him?"

"Why is he up here? Why is he so secretive? He is, isn't he? And you said it first. I mean, look, Spence, is Doe deaf and does he already know? Have he and his wife, Allison, known for a long time? And . . . if so — why did she let him take Doe? He said it was because she worked at night, and he has the summer off. But doesn't a deaf child need special help?"

Spencer turned in at the driveway to the Tavrow house. "Maybe," he suggested, "she didn't let him take Doe. In the paper, the paper from Minneapolis I was reading, there was this article. . . ."

Laurel felt annoyed. Spencer was changing the subject. She was trying to talk with him but he wasn't listening. He wanted to start discussing newspaper articles about motors or other mechanical gadgets. "What article?" she snapped. "This is important — really important."

"I know," he agreed, gliding up to her back door and stepping hard on the brakes. "There are, you know, worse things than just being deaf."

"Like?" she asked breathlessly. As she was speaking, it came to her. She knew. Suddenly everything made sense. "No — oh, no — don't say it. I saw the paper. I saw the article, too. About missing children — child-stealing. Like mothers stealing babies from fathers or fathers taking — oh, no, no, no. . . ."

TWENTY-ONE

Laurel fastened the brass chain on her back door. Then she watched Spencer jog toward his car. Even if it was the best solution, she didn't want him to leave. She was frightened to keep the baby at the empty house while he went to see Ivan.

When she could no longer see the VW, she went to check on Doe. Thumb in her mouth, the baby snuffled quietly as she slept on a sofa cushion in the bottom of the bathtub. The tub had been Spencer's idea. His various cousins had — occasionally — slept in tubs, he said. Bathtubs were safe places, he explained, if the main water values were shut off before the child was put in.

As Laurel crossed the bathroom floor to see whether Doe was warm enough, she tripped over a stool. It clattered against the tile floor. Laurel flinched, but the baby didn't stir.

"She's deaf. I know she is," Laurel said half aloud. The sound of her own voice soothed her nervousness. She wondered what Ivan would do when Spencer told him they knew he'd taken Doe from her mother. Would he agree to call Allison?

Thinking, Laurel moved from the bathroom to the living room. The house seemed unusually large. It creaked with unfamiliar noises. Shadows from the converted oil lamps hovered over her.

Spencer was going to get Ivan. The two of them would come to pick up Doe. That seemed simple enough. And yet, the more Laurel thought about the situation, the less happy she felt. Why should she return this baby to a man who had probably stolen her? If Doe needed special help, there was no sign Ivan would see that she got it.

Laurel was exhausted, but she couldn't sit in one place. She walked back and forth, inspecting Doe and every dark corner of the house. As she paced, she thought about the summer. In the last two months, Ivan had impressed her, won her over, made her love him. And then, of course, there was Doe. Although Laurel knew Doe needed to be protected, cherished, she was beginning to realize that she couldn't do it. The dream-Allison had put the kite into Laurel's hands without ever saying it was hers to keep. She was, after all, a sister, a daughter, but *not* a mother. In fact, she still needed a mother herself — even a critical or absentminded one.

The wind was blowing hard, whining through the stand of Norway pines that surrounded the house. Laurel looked out the front windows toward the lake. She scanned the sky for storm clouds but found none. Despite the wind, the sky was clear, strewn with faint stars. There was no moon, and the sky seemed to have an eerie brightness.

Shivering, Laurel resumed her pacing. Ivan, Allison, Laurel. Allison? Ivan? Doe needed love, but she needed care, too. And safety. An idea was forming inside Laurel's head. It was so simple she couldn't imagine why she hadn't thought of it before. The lights blinked. They blinked again. The wind was affecting the power lines strung through the woods. Laurel moved toward the telephone. After a moment, she sat down and dialed the operator.

"What's the area code for Minneapolis?" she asked.

A few seconds later, she had Minneapolis information on the line.

"What city do you want?" an operator asked crisply.

Laurel wasn't sure. "Minneapolis," she

suggested. "Ivan Wood," she said. "Or Allison Wood."

Laurel heard clicking noises. She held her breath. After what seemed like an interminable pause, the operator said, "Wood? W-O-O-D, Ivan or Allison. I'm sorry. I have no listing under either of those names."

"Try St. Paul," she said. But as she spoke, she already knew her idea was not going to work. There were dozens of suburbs in the Minneapolis–St. Paul area. She couldn't even be sure that Wood was his real name. Nor had he ever talked about exactly where he lived. Ivan, her friend, with whom she'd planned to spend the rest of her life. Where he lived, she realized, was one of many things he'd never discussed.

Discouraged, Laurel dropped the phone back into the cradle. She stood up. Then, heading for the bathroom, she checked once again on Doe. The child was sleeping peacefully. She was not disturbed by the gusty night wind. Laurel went back to the living room. She leaned her forehead against the front window and peered out toward the choppy shimmer of the lake.

Why hadn't she stayed at Jane's? Why had she decided to remain at the house? She had figured she'd only be there for a short while, but the time seemed endless. When the lights flickered again, she thought about going to the kitchen to hunt for candles, but she didn't. Instead, she squinted across the cove toward the trapper's cabin.

She saw nothing. There were no lights visible. At the same time, she listened for Spencer's car. Or even Miles's returning early. All she could hear, though, was the roar of the wind. Then, without warning, there was a flash, as heat lightning cut jaggedly across the sky over the lake.

As she watched, another flash illuminated the darkness. For a moment, it was as bright as midday. Laurel could see trees, path, beach, lake. Something else, too. A second later, everything was dark both outside and inside. The lightning was over, but the power was out.

It was so black inside that the front path seemed lit by more than stars. And running up the stone path was Ivan. As he ran, he shouted at her. At first, because of the wind, Laurel couldn't hear his words. His tone of voice, however, was unmistakable — angry, crazed. Intimidated, she jerked away from the window and cowered behind a chair.

Ivan pounded up the front steps. He banged the door, turned the handle. He pushed on it. Laurel held her breath. Because the door was bolted, all Ivan could do was rattle it.

"Open up," he screamed. "Laurel, open the door. I know you're in there. I saw you! Before you jumped back, I saw you! Now open up. Turn on the lights and unlock the door! I order you to do as I say."

Paralyzed by the fierceness of Ivan's tone, Laurel stood on the rag rug, feeling its braided roughness under her bare toes. She was afraid because the power was out, but she was grateful, too. Although Ivan had seen her, he could not see her now. For a moment, at least, she was protected by darkness and by the locked doors.

Ivan pounded again. "Laurel, Laurel, open up! Give me the baby!"

Laurel didn't move. She felt perspiration beading behind her ears and at the back of her knees. She stood in stunned silence, but Ivan kept banging and calling out to her. As long as he was at the door, she knew where he was. Although he was threatening her, he *was* outside. She knew she ought to take action, try to phone, hide. And yet she stood there.

For a while, Ivan's voice had the same frantic, out-of-control tone. But slowly it changed, began to plead, wheedle.

"Open up! Oh, you're clever — so clever. When I came in and found Doe gone, I didn't suspect you. I thought it was Allison," he explained.

Ivan pressed his face against the leaded-glass window next to the door. "I thought maybe Allison had found me, you see. So I had to go to town. I called her. Called and called and got no answer. All that time wasted in the phone booth thinking she was up here somewhere with Doe. But finally she answered. So I hung up, knowing she couldn't have been here and back to Minneapolis in a few hours' time. And then I knew. Laurel — you're listening. You are. Now answer me — answer me before I have to break in. Answer me! Answer me, you little brat."

Brat? Ivan had called her a little brat. Filled with a sudden surge of anger, she began to yell at him. "Go away! Get out of here. I'll call the police. My brother's coming back any minute. And besides, I . . . I have . . . a gun!"

Instead of sounding alarmed, Ivan laughed. His laugh was bitter, unfriendly. "What kind of a gun, little one? A pop gun, a water pistol? I don't believe you. You're bluffing. And you won't call the police, either. Because, if you did, you'd be in trouble for stealing my kid! Now, open the door, give me the baby."

Cautiously, Laurel moved toward one of

the front windows. She could see the outline of Ivan's form. The freak wind was subsiding so that his words sliced more clearly through the night. If she moved a few steps and unlocked the door, he could take Doe and be gone.

But she wouldn't do it. She felt responsible for Doe, for Doe's life and her health. She wasn't Allison, but until Allison could be found, she was taking her place.

"Laurel!"

"What?"

Ivan lowered his voice because he knew she was right on the other side of the window. "Open it. Open it before I have to break it in. I can, you know. I'll find an unlocked window. Or I'll just break one. Come on. Don't make it harder for both of us. This is not an adventure. Not a game. Now, be a good girl and open the door."

"No!"

Laurel knew what would come next. He wouldn't leave until he found a way to get in. As soon as she stopped talking to him, he'd circle the house. Circle and circle until. . . .

And then what? Laurel knew she could hide. She could protect herself by going into the tackle closet. As soon as she closed the door behind her, she could climb the shelves above the fishing gear, and in a few seconds she'd be into the crawl space. She'd be safe. Ivan would never find her there. But Doe — Doe wouldn't be safe. He'd steal his daughter from the bathtub and run off somewhere else.

"Go away," Laurel told him, knowing she was brave for Doe's sake and not for her own. She felt like a wild animal protecting her young. "Go away. I'll bring her back in the morning."

TWENTY-TWO

Because the wind had died down, everything was quiet outside. Although the power was still off, it might flash on again any moment. Laurel looked around for a weapon. On the wall was an Indian bow and arrow, an Indian tomahawk. She reached out toward the toma-hawk. It was wooden, but better than noth-ing. She didn't care what Ivan said, what he did, she was going to protect Doe, who shouldn't be dragged secretly from place to place. Allison had a right to her daughter, too. And Doe, if she was deaf, deserved to have help.

"Go away, Ivan! Go away, I tell you!"

Instead of doing as she said, Ivan stayed by the leaded-glass window. Laurel could see him clearly now because it seemed to be getting brighter outside, almost as if it were morning instead of the middle of the night.

"Laurel, come on. Can't you understand my pain? I'm not Job. I don't have his resigned outlook to fate. How do you think I felt when I found that empty crib? Come now — where's my baby?"

Laurel leaned her forehead against the windowpane. Ivan's voice didn't calm her. It made her feel close to hysteria. She closed her eyes. Instead of feeling better, she felt worse as kite images exploded behind her closed lids. No, not images, but *an* image of a luminous shape pitching and rolling at the end of its fragile tether. Words spun turbulently through her head.

Then, almost involuntarily, they began to spill out. "What about Allison?" she asked, opening her eyes. "How did she feel when the phone rang tonight and then no one was there? Where does Allison think her baby is? How did she feel when she found the empty crib? And what about Doe? Doesn't she deserve something better?"

Ivan stopped pounding. "She's not your baby," he answered. "Not your problem."

"Oh, yes — yes — now it is. Now that I love Doe. Now that I'm worried she can't hear. That's why I took her to Jane. That's why — "

"To Jane Collier? You took her to a doctor? Why should Jane see her? Doe's fine. *I'm* taking care of her. *I'm* doing what she needs. Why did you have to butt in? I should have known. All I wanted was a baby-sitter. But you weren't right. Weren't ever right. You're just a child."

Ivan's face was in the shadows. It was a few inches from hers. Only a pane of glass separated them. Laurel wanted to shrink back, but she forced herself to stand there where she could protect the baby if he tried to break in. Besides, she heard a gravel noise from somewhere behind the house which made her feel braver.

Ivan's insults were startling yet revealing. As she listened, she *was* bratty little Laurel Tavrow standing there in her cutoffs and bare feet, but she was someone else, too. Part of her hovered overhead watching the scene unfold at the house on Hoop Lake.

At this moment, she saw Ivan differently than she ever had before. He was calling her a child when he was still some kind of child, looking for games and excitement. Kidnapping his own daughter. Pretending she wasn't unusual.

"Let me in, Laurel. Before I have to do something drastic. I want my baby."

Laurel was numb. "Doesn't Allison want her, too?"

Whether Doe was deaf or not, there was a

problem. Doe needed attention she could not get at an isolated cabin in Minnesota. It didn't matter how much Ivan loved her. Sometimes loving wasn't enough.

"Laurel, I am not listening to you. I am not listening!"

Ivan's tone should have deflated her courage, but she could hear the grating sound of Miles's tires. Laurel wasn't alone anymore. Now that her brother had arrived, everything would be all right.

"Go away, Ivan. I'm not listening, either. It's too late. Too late, and you can't have her — "

She stopped in mid-sentence and took a deep breath. Where was Miles? Ivan didn't seem to have heard a car. Maybe she had been wrong. But she did have an idea. If she lied to Ivan, told him a convincing lie, he might go away.

"Ivan . . . listen. Doe's not here."

"Yes, she is!"

Laurel twisted her hands together. "No, no — she's not."

"Then where is she?" Ivan demanded.

"I've left her somewhere else tonight. You can have her tomorrow."

"Tomorrow?"

"Yes" — Laurel told him — "tomorrow . . . after you've called Allison."

Ivan ignored her statement. "Is she at the Harrisons'? Or at Jane Collier's? I'll find her there. Now — tonight. I must know where she is!"

Laurel leaned her head against the window. As she thought about the lie she was going to tell, she examined Ivan. He looked wretched. Laurel felt sorry for him, but she didn't feel forgiving.

"Laurel, out with it. Where is my baby?"

"With the nuns," she said.

"Where?"

"With the nuns," Laurel repeated, trying to use a stronger, more convincing tone. "So, if you want her, go rattle their doors."

"The nuns?" Ivan repeated dully. "You left my daughter with them? What do nuns know about babies?"

"What do I know about babies? What do you know?"

Streaks of light were rising in the western sky almost as if there were a fire over toward Fishhook Lake. She could see Ivan clearly now, and behind Ivan, leaning against the well, she could see, not her brother, but Spencer.

Ivan glared at her. "I'm going to get my daughter from the nuns. Then I'm going to come back here, Laurel. I'm going to break into your place and paddle you so hard you won't be able to sit down for a month!"

Laurel slid the tomahawk back and forth in her hands. Spencer was as good as Miles. Spencer wouldn't let Ivan hurt her. "Go on," she dared him. "Go rattle the doors at the nuns' lodge. They lock their windows, Ivan. They bolt their doors. When they hear your voice, Ivan, threatening them, they'll call the police. And you'll never get your daughter back then. Never, Ivan. It will always be like it is now."

Instead of feeling young and weak, she felt powerful. She put down the tomahawk. She didn't need it. Ivan wasn't brave. Who but a coward would steal his own child and try to hide out with her? Spencer was still standing by the well. It was good to know he was there, but she was all right. Ivan was not going to break into her house.

Laurel looked beyond him to the lake and the sky. Bright fingers of light streaked across the horizon. The stars were no longer visible because the sky beyond Ivan was radiant. Wind and heat lightning had been replaced by an array of northern lights.

She'd longed for them that night in the cove when she'd been so in love with Ivan. Now, when she wanted to forget, they had appeared. Watching the flares of light, she realized that it must be close to midnight.

Close to the beginning of her fourteenth birthday. She might be fourteen, but she was not yet ready to see northern lights with a man, a lover. If her mother were here, she'd tell Laurel that in no uncertain terms. And she'd also say that Laurel was not old enough to have half the responsibility for a baby — even if that baby didn't need special care.

"Go away," she urged Ivan again. "I'll see you in the morning." She didn't hate Ivan, but she was determined to do the best possible thing for Doe.

"I'll see you in the morning. Tomorrow," she promised, pressing one palm against the glass. Ivan matched his larger hand against hers. Stunned by an unexpected surge of emotion, she drew her hand away. Then, without looking back, she crossed through the living room and scurried toward the bathroom.

When she got there, she knelt by the tub. In the darkness, she watched the sleeping child and tried to keep her head clear of all thoughts.

TWENTY-THREE

Even before Laurel saw Ivan, she heard the sound of the grindstone. When she reached the clearing, she found him on the front porch of the cabin bent over a table. Gouges and chisels were everywhere. He also had a pan of water and a can of oil. Each time he pressed a tool against one of the moving wheels, he sent showers of sparks in all directions.

Ivan was so absorbed, he didn't seem to know she was there. She had expected him to be pacing anxiously as he waited for her to bring Doe. Instead, as if he didn't have a care in the world, he was sharpening tools. After a while, he pulled back from the stone. His gouge made a hissing sound as he cooled it in the pan.

"I'm putting a new bevel on this one," he

explained without looking up. "On a curved surface, it's a devil of a job."

Laurel nodded wordlessly. Feeling edgy, she moved forward and seated herself on one side of the porch. She faced the lake. Her legs dangled loosely, but her hands were clenched into fists. Digging her nails into her palms, she tried to figure out what game Ivan was playing this morning.

Whatever it was, he was in no hurry. He began to use the grindstone again. After a few moments, Laurel realized that she wasn't in a hurry, either. Doe was safe. She was being loved and looked after, so Laurel had the whole morning. Or all day for that matter. She pulled a comb from her pocket. She unfastened her hair. Then, patiently, she combed out tangles and rebraided it. As she sat there working on her hair, she could feel her tension dissolve.

At one end of the cove, a fish jumped. Then another. Ivan continued to sharpen his tools. After what seemed like hours, Laurel slid off the porch. If Ivan wasn't going to talk, she didn't intend to stay. She was going to follow the shoreline back to her house. Maybe Miles — who'd been delayed last night by car trouble — had returned by now.

As she started downhill toward the lake,

the grindstone stopped. "Hey, wait," Ivan called.

Laurel paused, but she didn't turn to look at him.

"Where's Doe?" he asked. "You promised to bring her."

"I didn't," Laurel said.

"Where is she?"

"With the nuns." Last night that had not been a truthful answer, but this morning it was. She and Spencer had decided that Doe needed real safety. Doe shouldn't go back to Ivan until he let Allison know where he was, until he promised to have the baby's hearing checked.

The nuns had not needed much persuasion. They, too, felt that they wanted to be sure Doe's mother knew where she was. Therefore, they had agreed to care for her until someone reached Allison. Although Sister Inez planned to drive over and speak with Ivan, Laurel had arrived first. Now she wondered if she had made a mistake.

"Laurel," Ivan called softly. "Come back. Let's talk. I got out the tools to take my mind off things. And also . . . because I don't think I'm going to be here much longer."

Laurel balanced on one foot. He sounded reasonable and sincere. He wasn't angry that she hadn't brought the baby to him. He seemed to understand what she had in mind.

"Come back, honey — please."

Laurel turned. She nodded. Feeling shaky, she returned to her place at the corner of the porch. Ivan sat down next to her. "How's Doe?" he asked. "Have you seen her today? Does she miss me?"

"Yes, I gave her breakfast — cereal, juice out of a cup. She had a piece of toast, too, but when she got tired of it, she tore it to bits. And yes, she's very, very serious today. She does miss you."

"Laurel?"

"What?"

"I'm sorry about last night. When Doe was missing, I went berserk. By the time I got to your place, I was distraught. With the weather and all, it was like the mad scene from *Lear*. Or maybe not *Lear* but *The Tempest*. I was acting like Caliban. Or like I was crazy."

Laurel drew her knees up to her chest. She picked at a scab on her right shin. "So was I. How could I have taken her? I must have been crazy, too. Worrying about her made us both that way." Pausing, she rubbed at one eye. She had something else to say. She was not sure Ivan would continue to be so calm and pleasant when she said it. "Ivan?"

"What?"

"Allison must be crazy, too. It's been weeks. Call her now. Please, Ivan."

Although Ivan nodded, he looked preoccupied. "What's the date today? It must be the sixteenth or almost the sixteenth," he mused. "Allison's birthday. You're right, of course. I'll tell her where we are."

Ivan remembered Allison's birthday but not hers. Laurel glanced in his direction. But he wasn't looking at her. He was gazing into the branches of the maple that stood beside the cabin. "Yes . . ." he mused. "I must call."

Spencer had been wrong to think Laurel needed help. This was going to be easy. After she had worried so much, Ivan had agreed immediately.

He didn't move, however. As Laurel watched, he sharpened the tip of another gouge. She began to feel irritated, impatient. "What are we waiting for? Let's go to the Harrisons' and use the telephone."

"We will," Ivan agreed. "I need a little time to think and to pull myself together."

"Mmm," Laurel answered. She understood, but — still — she wanted him to talk to Allison. "Ivan?"

"Hmmm?"

"Is Wood your real name?"

"Of course."

"And where do you live?"

"Edina," he answered without hesitation. He stared up into the tree. "In an apartment over a drugstore. I'll call Allison, give her a birthday present. But, Laurel, first — before we call — one last thing."

"What?"

"Let's climb the tree. Ever since I came I've wanted to do that."

Vexed, Laurel shook her head. This was another game. Ivan knew what it was because it was *his* game. But Laurel didn't. At least not yet. "No . . ." she said.

"Let's climb. Now," Ivan urged.

Laurel shook her head. "No, you need to telephone Doe's mother. Besides, I don't like to climb trees."

"You wouldn't," Ivan said, springing to his feet. "You're always cautious — too cautious. Oh, you've freed up a lot this summer, but you have a long way to go."

As Ivan spoke, he took hold of Laurel's hands and pulled her to her feet. "So come on, I'll give you a boost."

Laurel laughed nervously. Against her will and her judgment, she was about to let Ivan draw her into his game. "No, not me," she replied, pulling away.

"Yes — you — now." Then, before she had

time to resist, he boosted her from the porch railing into the lowest fork of the tree. The bark was rough against her bare arms and legs.

"Higher," Ivan urged. "Move up and make some room for me."

Laurel clutched the trunk as she tried to do what Ivan told her. He scrambled from the railing into the maple. Quickly he brushed by. Using his arms to haul himself higher, he climbed into the branches above her head.

She peered between the leaves out toward the lake. Leaves, lake, sun. It looked like a glorious patchwork quilt. She glanced up toward Ivan.

He was looking at her. "Come here. Near me," he called. "I need you. Here. There's something important I need to tell you."

"I can't," Laurel told him. "I'm afraid."

"Don't be, sweetheart. I'm here. I won't let anything happen to you. Just take it slowly. You are strong and brave. You're Joan of Arc. You're Florence Nightingale. You're Miranda. If you don't know that after last night, you'll never know it."

Ivan's tone made Laurel feel warm. Responding to it, she inched higher toward the fork where he sat. Soon she was right below him. Then, once he had steadied her, she was opposite him. They were swaying together near the crest of the maple tree. They were above the roof of the cabin.

"Now," Ivan whispered breathlessly. "Look."

Laurel scanned Hoop Lake, glimpsing her house, then the nuns' lodge. She was uneasy. She didn't feel safe. She had liked it better when she was quilted in with leaves. Now she was dangerously high, unprotected. She was also too close to Ivan. His gray eyes examined her as if she were a block of wood that he was about to carve.

She looked down. Her stomach lurched. "Too high," she murmured. "Got to get out of here."

Ivan reached out and took hold of her arm. "No."

She felt panicky. She wanted to move away, but her position was precarious. "What is it? You said you wanted to talk." Her voice was faint. She didn't want to meet Ivan's eyes, but it was impossible to avoid them.

"Laurel honey. . . ."

Her stomach lurched again. "What?"

"Let's go away together. Just you and me and Doe. Wait — don't speak yet. Hear me out, let me finish. We can take care of Doe. The three of us can live together. Doesn't that sound wonderful? Canada maybe — would you like that? I can always get work as a carpenter, you know."

Darts of pain pinched her arms, her legs, her chest. "But what about Allison?" she asked.

"We'll call her and work something out, won't we? Isn't that the way you want it? The way we both want it? It's over between Allison and me, you know that, don't you? And look, Laurel, I care about you. I love you as I love Doe. You — even if you don't always see it — are a very special person."

Over and over Laurel had dreamed of hearing Ivan speak to her this way. She wanted to be grown-up, wanted to be safe — loved and cared for. But now that it was actually happening, it was wrong. She pulled back. "Let go of my arm," she said.

Ivan did as she asked. "Sorry, love. I didn't mean to hurt you. You're dear to me, like some perfect crystal I've found in a dark cave. All you need to shine brilliantly is to be brought up to the light and polished a bit. I want you with me — with me and with Doe. Besides, I thought you cared for me."

She did. She cared for him and more. She *loved* him, but at the same time she hated him. This was not happening. It was a dream or some kind of nightmare. She was going to wake up back in the house with Doe still asleep in the bathtub.

Her left foot prickled. The swaying motion of the tree lulled her. Then Ivan reached out and touched her forehead with the tip of his index finger. "Stop scowling. Stop worrying."

"No," she said softly. "This isn't a dream."

"Of course it isn't," Ivan responded. "It's real, and we both want the same thing."

"I don't think so," Laurel said, suddenly aware that she was no longer afraid to speak up to Ivan. "What about testing for Doe?"

Ivan frowned. "Sometimes, my pet, you sound like Allison. I appreciate you more when you're your own sweet, unself-conscious self."

Laurel had to climb down out of the tree. She wanted to get away. "Ivan?"

"What?"

"Tell me something."

"Sure."

"Why did you run away with Doe?"

Ivan stroked his beard. Then, squinting, he answered. "Because she — Allison — intended to take her from me. Whether I liked it or not, she said. And I'd never see Doe again. She said I had my head in the sand and didn't deserve to be a husband or a father. She was going to move with Doe to a place with a special program for the deaf."

Laurel nodded. Everything was starting to make sense. Not just what Ivan was saying, but what he was withholding. At last she understood the game. "Then you *knew*. You knew the whole time. Before the wasp, too."

"Yes and no. Allison said so, but she was wrong. There's nothing the matter with Doe. She's just a late bloomer. And I like late bloomers — like you, for instance." Ivan's statement was accompanied by another smile.

Laurel shifted so she was a few inches farther from where he sat. A squeezing sensation in her chest made it hard to breathe. Last night, she reminded herself, she had been "brat" and last week just the baby-sitter. "What about Jessica?" she asked abruptly.

"What about her?"

"Isn't Jessica special to you?"

"Jealous?" Ivan asked. "Are you jealous? Why, I'm flattered. But there's no need. Jessica doesn't want to be burdened with me or with a baby. She's going places, that Jessica, and those places don't include dreamers like us, pet. Besides, she's not exactly a Galatea. Every sculptor fancies himself a Pygmalion searching for his Galatea. You're closer to it — much closer. Fine bones, quizzical eyes. And an aura — a whole world of promise and potential waiting to be chipped out of the pith."

The pain was so intense that Laurel knew she couldn't stay in the tree even a minute longer. Groping for secure footholds, she began to work her way down.

"Hey, wait," Ivan said. "We're talking, and it's beautiful here. It's a crow's nest, and we're two pirates surveying the seven seas. Look, see the nuns out on their pontoon raft. Maybe Doe's riding with them. Having a day's holiday from her isn't half bad, you know. Because I worry so much. I'm always worrying. But I like being with you. I do, Laurel. Laurel — stop!"

Laurel heard Ivan's words, but she didn't listen to him. She slid one foot and then another foot below her from one V to another on her way down to the ground.

"Laurel, don't. Where are you going? Don't you want to stay with Doe and me?"

Laurel swung herself over the last branch and stretched out to steady herself on the porch railing. At last she knew why this conversation had such an unreal feeling. Because it was unreal. Because it was a lie.

Ivan didn't want her. The game he was playing this morning was called Fool Laurel. Laurel the fool. Fool her into thinking she's wanted, she's important. Lull her into agreeing to make plans to flee, into bringing back the baby. All Ivan needed was a little time. Time to pack up. Because he was going to leave. Leave with Doe and without Laurel.

She — Laurel — was nothing to him. Only what she'd seen the week Jessica had been around. Laurel the baby-sitter. Ivan's proposal was a fake. He was stalling, figuring how much he could get done before he fled. That's why he had been sharpening tools, too. Part of his preparation. He wasn't really relaxed, really tender. He was plotting, planning. In a few hours, he'd disappear, leaving Laurel behind forever. And meanwhile, Allison would still not know where her daughter was.

"Laurel!" Ivan called sharply as he heard her feet hit the boards of the porch. "Stop! Where are you going?"

"To make a phone call." Laurel stepped off the porch and headed back away from the lake. "To Edina," she said. "To tell Allison that she can meet Doe and you at the nuns' lodge on Hoop Lake."

Ivan was silent. He didn't call out or plead with her. Laurel was surprised, but she didn't stop to ask questions. She hoped the name was Wood and that the phone number was listed with information. Last night she'd seen he was a coward, yet today — for a while — she'd forgotten. Well, she wouldn't forget again.

Picking up a stone, Laurel aimed at the trunk of a pine tree. "Bull's-eye," she said as she hurried after it. She wanted to be complimented, to be loved, to hear tender words whispered in her ear. But she wanted it to be real, not make-believe. She hurt. And for a long time, the hurt would keep reminding her of Ivan — of how she felt about him and he had never felt about her.

And Allison? Had Ivan ever loved *her*? Laurel didn't know, but she did know that she was going to make that telephone call. What was Allison like? Weak? Strong? Laurel hoped that she was strong, wise, and caring, like the dream-Allison. But it was only a hope.

Maybe, while Laurel was at it, she'd place a call to her own mother. Tell her that Sri Lanka was too far away, that she needed more of the right kind of attention. In any case, Laurel was on her way. She would tell Allison where to find her baby. This was a birthday present, a real, unforgettable birthday present.

TWENTY-FOUR

Laurel crunched leaves beneath her feet. She sniffed. The early-morning air was cool. Goldenrod pollen made her nose itch. Fall was coming. It was still August, but soon it would be September.

As she walked through the woods, her eyes scanned the trees — pine, aspen, birch, apple. They were only trees now. Their Druid spirits had blown away. Naming trees and playing games were for younger girls. This morning she felt old. What she couldn't understand was how a person could feel old without feeling grown-up. When her parents arrived, would they — especially her mother — see how she had changed? Well, Laurel would make her see, make her listen.

Moving with determination, Laurel marched along the well-worn path toward the trapper's cabin. She didn't want to go, yet she forced herself. "One foot, other foot," she whispered. "One last time. . . ."

Shafts of light filtered down through the trees. Wild canaries sang from a copse. A damp spiderweb sagged and clung to her face. As Laurel brushed it aside, she tried to remember June, July, and August. She wanted to hold the days and weeks in her head, peeling them off one by one like layers of curling birch bark. Doe — loving Doe. Ivan — loving Ivan. Losing Doe, losing Ivan.

Thinking about them made notes of music swell inside her head. Then she heard music around her drifting through the trees. It wasn't wild canaries but violins, playing a piece so sweet, so sad, that Laurel felt like dancing a slow, rhythmic dance. But the music was not inside her head. It was not imaginary. It was real. Even the birds, heads cocked, were listening.

Laurel stopped and looked around. Spencer. This was his doing. She'd set off another one of his electric eyes. Somewhere behind her were wires and a tape deck. Instead of laughter or the cries of crazed loons, her steps had turned on a symphony. Resentful, she wondered how Spencer could play a joke this morning of all mornings.

She looked around, but to her surprise, she did not see him hidden in the underbrush. He did not jump out to nag or tease. She was alone with the music, and the violins were so sweet she could feel tears salt her eyes.

Something silken floated by. It looked like a tiny ballerina, but it was a milkweed seed. Then another bobbed by, and another. Watching them, Laurel forgot about being annoyed. She turned, looking for the plant. When she spotted it, she reached forward and tugged. The open pods released waves of dancers who glided through the air in time to the music. Laurel tore off a length of vine and wrapped it around her shoulders. The woods teemed with miniature dancers. They waltzed and Laurel — though she knew nothing of dancing — waltzed with them.

She spun on the path and off it, through grass and wildflowers and patches of red-tinged poison ivy. But she kept moving toward the cabin. The music, with its high, piercing tones, followed her. It grew softer yet no less distinct. She could hear each note as she could see each day with Ivan and with Doe. Maybe Spencer, for once, was not playing a joke.

As Laurel approached the clearing, the music began to accelerate, racing toward a frantic conclusion. Listening intently, she paused. Her body was loose and languid. Then, abruptly, the music stopped. Everything was silent once again. All she heard was a breeze ruffling the aspens and the cries of distant jays.

For a moment she stood in the shade. Stood as she had many times, watching Ivan. Around her she felt shadows, a sense of mystery and of loss. Laurel wanted to step forward, but she was afraid.

At last, she forced herself to walk forward into the glaring sunlight. Haltingly, she skirted the edge of the cabin and moved around to the front. The yard was littered with curved chips of wood. A chisel gleamed in the sunlight. Laurel bent down and took hold of it. It was broken. The rasp next to it was dull and rusted.

Wary of approaching the cabin, she sat on the edge of the stump. The door was ajar. Lumpy green garbage bags lay on the porch with flies buzzing above them. Only Ivan could pile them there without bothering to close the tops. She picked up the rasp. She placed it and the chisel neatly beside her.

Then, taking a deep breath, she stood and moved toward the cabin. It was empty. Ivan was gone. Doe was gone, too. The nuns had reached Allison. By the time Allison had arrived, Ivan had packed his things into his trunk and driven off. North, Spencer said. Ivan was alone and heading north. Without

Doe. Without Laurel. She felt sad. For herself, for Ivan. But sad for Allison and for Doe, too.

A torn T-shirt lay on the steps. Laurel bent down for it. The shirt smelled of paint thinner and glue. It smelled of Ivan. Distressed, she flung it on top of the garbage bags. She kicked at one of Doe's old blocks. "P, Q, R," it said. She hugged her arms across her chest. She was only a foot from the front door, but she didn't want to reach out and touch it.

Finally, however, swallowing her fear, she pushed at the door with one foot. It squealed. Ivan never had gotten around to oiling the hinges. She kicked again, and it swung open. For a moment, at the threshold, she hesitated. Then she willed herself to move forward into the cabin's shadowy interior. The curtains were drawn and the windows closed. Already, in less than a day, the cabin had begun to take on a musty, abandoned, winter smell.

On the floor at her feet lay the broom. She bent over and took hold of it. Ivan had made a halfhearted attempt to sweep up, but he hadn't gotten as far as using a dustpan or putting the broom back in the corner next to the sink. Laurel's nose told her that somewhere there was a wet diaper which had not been thrown away. Ivan's mattress was stripped and ugly. The side of the wooden crib hung down as though Doe had escaped by herself and crawled away.

They were gone, and yet at the same time the cabin was so littered with discarded clothes and sheets that it might have been washday. When Laurel held her breath, she could imagine Ivan bounding in at the back door with Doe propped jauntily on one hip.

Turning, Laurel wandered into the kitchen. The linoleum floor was greasy. In the sink were dishes with yesterday's food sticking to them. A glass of soured milk sat on top of the refrigerator. Absentmindedly, Laurel shook the detergent bottle, which stood on a shelf next to the half-empty can of wax.

She considered running a sinkful of water, washing, sweeping, tying the tops of the garbage bags. It seemed almost as if that were her job, as if Ivan had thrown up his hands and left it all for her to do. If she didn't clean the cabin, then Spencer and Annie Harrison would have to do it. Because Ivan wasn't coming back. She wasn't ever going to see him again.

Ivan — so wonderful and at the same time so terrible. Brave yet cowardly. Grown-up yet childlike. Laurel couldn't make sense of him or of anything. Had Spencer been right when he said she had a crush on Ivan? No, he'd been wrong. A thirteen- or fourteen-year-old *was* capable of feeling love. "Yes," she told herself. Yes — even if her plans had been make-believe, like something out of Druidworld — her feelings were real. And that's why she still hurt so much.

As she reached to put the broom back where it belonged, tears began to glaze her eyes. Through them, she saw Doe's sun hat lying on a shelf next to two cans of fruit cocktail. It was crumpled, rust-stained. Someone, getting Doe a cookie, had dropped the hat there and forgotten it. When Laurel held it to her nose, she smelled the sweet baby scents of talcum and sweat. She swiped at her eyes. Then she sniffed at the hat again.

As she did, she remembered the melody of Spencer's violin music, and new tears welled up in her eyes. Because Laurel had been afraid, terrified that the real Allison wouldn't be as wonderful as she had imagined, she hadn't gone to see her when she had come for Doe. Now Laurel was worried. Was Allison as loving and careful of the baby as she had been? Would Doe be all right?

Undecided, Laurel turned from the sink and looked across the cabin. Then she put her hands in her pockets. She didn't intend to do the dishes or clean. She was sorry there was so much work left for the Harrisons, but she wasn't the one that had rented the cabin to Ivan.

Sighing, she started toward the door. Yet as she moved, something attracted her glance. It was only a rag left in the middle of the dining table, but it bulged intriguingly. Laurel stepped sideways and reached out. She touched the rag. It was damp. Something angular lay beneath it.

For a long while, she stood rooted to the spot. Then finally, summoning her courage, she snatched the rag away. There on the table she saw a mound of damp clay. It was a model for one of Ivan's sculptures. Laurel dropped the rag. Clenching and unclenching her fists, she moved closer.

She was looking at a small, deftly shaped figure of a girl — a pensive girl holding her knees under her chin. The girl looked as if she was poised that way just for a moment, seemed as if she was going to spring to her feet and flee at any instant. Laurel's breath came in ragged little bursts. That girl of clay had a French braid over the top of her head. In one hand she had a hat — a baby's sun hat. And there was something on her knee. Laurel squinted. It was hardly more than a bit of clay. Yet, at the same time, it was a butterfly, a minute butterfly.

Slowly, Laurel moved around the table, examining the sculpture from all angles. At second glance, she realized that it — like everything Ivan ever did — was half finished. The feet were undefined, merging into the lumpy clay of the base. One hand had only four fingers. One leg seemed to be wearing shorts while the other was bare. Unfinished. Like she felt.

He had left it behind, too. The clay pieces were models for his wooden ones. He had left this like the old rasp and broken chisel. It was not important and no longer interested him. He would never take a piece of walnut or black locust and chip it into a girl with a butterfly on one knee. Or would he? She had seen Ivan create ideas out of clay and squash them down, then — from memory — begin to carve the same image in a block of wood. She touched the clay. Her finger left a print in the girl's soft back.

Stepping away, she surveyed the room again. Everything in it had a hurried, messy, haphazard look — everything except the small sculpture. Why had Ivan left it on the table? Why had he covered it instead of smashing it back into his plastic bag filled with clay?

Had he, perhaps, left it there for Laurel? As a way of saying something about how he felt about her? She didn't know, couldn't decide. Ivan was too simple and too complex. She often had trouble figuring out what he had in mind. And yet, this time she thought she knew.

This was an offering, a statement. Instead of writing her a message, he'd left something else. "Should I take it?" she asked herself. Would she accept this token? She wasn't sure. Looking at it made her throat dry, her stomach tighten. Was she that girl? To Ivan, did she look that lovely, that special?

If she left it, it would probably be tossed out with the debris. Neither Spencer nor his mother would see anything there but a lump of clay. And that would be it. No souvenir of the summer, not even a photograph. Laurel bent and retrieved the rag. Thinking hard, she twisted it in her hands. Then, pursing her lips, she dropped the rag back over the clay figure.

She wanted to think. She'd decide later. Right now there was something else she wanted to do. Resolutely, she turned away and walked out the door. She headed toward the lake. She was almost there when suddenly Spencer jumped down from the roof of the shed and landed at her feet.

"Surprise," he cried. "I see old Ivan's flown the coop. He really was a jerk, wasn't he? Did you like the music this morning? I thought you would. I mean — I wanted — "

"Wanted what?" Laurel snapped.

"Wanted to cheer you up. Get you into a better mood."

"Better than what?"

"Than you felt about losing him and the kid, too. Say, that Allison's a dish. I was there, you know, when she picked up the baby." As Spencer spoke, he gestured with his hands to make sure Laurel understood. "Dishy, but with a sad-looking face. She said she's a nurse, and I guess that's what nurses always look like. At least, if I'm sick I'd like my nurse to — "

"Shut up, Spencer," Laurel said.

"Hey, that's not nice. And after all I did for you. Where would you be, and that precious baby you think so much of, if I hadn't helped? Child stealing can be a crime, you know. Ivan's wife could have called in the police."

"Did she?" Laurel asked.

"No, she said she wouldn't. That she was just glad to see her baby. If you'd showed up to meet her, you'd have known all that. Why didn't you? Why not?"

"Well . . ." Laurel said.

"Yeah, well, I guess I see. I mean, you were sweet on that guy before I started to show you what a jerk he was. You sure were moony, like a lovesick calf, like — "

She should have been angry with Spencer. Instead, she felt only mildly irritated, as if he were a mosquito and she were about to swat at him. For a moment she closed her eyes. She pictured the sculpture again. Then she tried to summon up Ivan's face and Doe's. "Shut up, Spence."

"Awe, come on, Pokey, you don't mean that. I'm trusty Spencer, the faithful sidekick, always at the ready. I looked after you. Kept an eye out to keep you out of trouble. So, hey, don't I get appreciation? Don't I get any reward for faithfulness and service in and out of the line of duty?"

Laurel listened to what he was saying. He was wrong. He didn't understand anything. But then again, he was right, of course. And she wasn't really upset. After all, he couldn't help being Spencer. Nothing, absolutely nothing, could transform him into King Tarik. "Mmm . . ." she said.

"About my reward," Spencer declared.

"What about it?"

"I've come to claim it now. I mean, we've solved the case, returned the kid to her rightful owner. It's some job we've done this summer. And now I think it's time to claim my just reward."

"And what," Laurel asked, matching her tone to his, "is your just reward, sir?"

"A night together. A night we'll never forget."

Laurel sighed. "What kind of night?"

Spencer fell to his knees. "Just the two of us, Laurel. A night at the drive-in."

"Mmm . . ." she replied, looking at Spencer but thinking once again of the tiny sculpture.

Spencer flung out his arms. "Come on, please. They have popcorn like Styrofoam and pizza that tastes like old socks."

"No . . . no, I don't think so," she said, speaking in a soft voice.

"But why?" he asked.

For a moment Laurel stood there frowning. Then, impulsively, she leaned forward and kissed him on top of his head. He smelled doggy. "Listen, Spence, I think you should forget about me and the drive-in this summer. Because — right now, at least — this thing between us just isn't going to work. . . ."

As Laurel's voice trailed off, she edged past Spencer and sprinted toward the canoe which Ivan had left at the water's edge. By the time Spencer had reached the sand, she had pushed off. Paddling alone, she headed out from shore.

He called to her, but she didn't answer. She concentrated until she could hear nothing except the lapping of waves against the side of the canoe and the drip, drip, drip as she feathered her paddle. When she looked back, she saw small whirlpools spinning behind the boat. She felt strong as she stroked away from the beach, strong and sure. She was going to skim the edge of the sandbar. As the sun rose above the trees, she would be paddling across Hoop Lake. Paddling and thinking. Trying to decide how she felt, who she was, whether she would go back to pick up the token Ivan had left behind.

Slowly, carefully, she threaded her way through the cattails until she was out of the shadows and into a wedge of sunlight that stretched as far as she could see.

About the Author

Susan Terris is a graduate of Wellesley College and holds a masters degree in English Literature from San Francisco State University. She is the author of over a dozen books for young readers and has reviewed children's books in *The New York Times*. Ms. Terris also teaches writing workshops at the University of California, Berkeley. She lives in San Francisco.